Mogul and Me

Mogul and Me

Peter Cumming

illustrations by
P. John Burden

*For the students
of Shakespeare School*

*Peter Cumming
Stratford
May 1995*

Ragweed Press
Charlottetown
1989

Text © 1989 by Peter Cumming
Illustration © by P. John Burden
ISBN 0-920304-82-6

Second Printing, 1991

Book Design by Cape Bear Associates
Printed and Bound in Canada
by Gagné Printing

Published by
Ragweed Press
P.O. Box 2023
Charlottetown, PEI, Canada
C1A 7N7

With thanks to the Canada Council for its generous support.

The author gratefully acknowledges research assistance by
Helen Russell and an Ontario Arts Council grant which
allowed him to begin the work on this book.

Canadian Cataloguing in Publication Data
Cumming, Peter, 1951-

Mogul and me
ISBN 0-920304-82-6

1. Elephants — Juvenile fiction.
I. Burden, P. John, 1942-   II. Title.

PS8555.U45M63 1898   jC813'.54   C89-098652-5
PZ10.3.C85Mo 1989

Printed on paper
containing over 50%
recycled paper including
5% post-consumer fibre.

For Ross and Alice...
their love of history
their love of books
their love of life

Chapter One

The first time I saw my elephant, he was nothing but a picture on a poster on a tree.

My father and I were cutting wood at the back of our farm, by the road that winds through the forest up along the river on its way to Saint John, New Brunswick, here in British North America.

Pa was chopping down trees to help us finish our new square-timbered house. After felling each log, he was trimming the branches with his axe. My horse and I were dragging the logs out of the woods onto the hard-packed dirt road.

It seems to me now, that on that sunny, cool October day of 1836, time and my life were plodding along like my horse—not waiting for or expecting anything out of the ordinary. Never in my wildest dreams did I imagine that something magic would come into my life that day and turn my living right around.

But as I came out of the darkness of the forest onto the sun-spangled road, I realized at once that something had changed in my quiet corner of the world. Though I had heard no hoofbeats, dust from some passing horse hung heavily in the air. And on the other side of the road, in those silent woods far from any other living soul, there was a large poster nailed to the trunk of a pine tree.

From what place had this waybill come? I wondered.

I unhitched a log and I and my horse walked across the road to the tree.

Who had brought this sign here to my quiet home? What did the poster say? What might it have to do with me?

The only sound that broke the stillness of the autumn day was the steady chopping of my father's axe. Then even the axe stopped.

"Halloo! Where are you, Son?" my father's voice rang out.

I heard but did not hear my father call me from the woods. Already I was lost in the poster on the tree.

My horse nuzzled her big nose into my shoulder, impatient to get back to work. But I had eyes only for the picture come here to my humble home as if from some other world.

Carefully I reached out to touch the poster. I fingered the black letters of every shape and size on the waybill and wondered what the strange words said. I ran my hand around the edge of the poster, along a border of wildflowers like those my mother used to pick. I traced the outline of the wonderful picture in the centre of the poster.

"I've cut another tree! Come get it, Son!" the voice of my father called. If I heard my father, I showed no sign. My mind was a million miles away, wrapped up as I was in my dreams.

There, in the picture on the tree on the quiet old road outside the small city of Saint John, on that day in fall so many years ago, was an elephant...a huge wonderful circus elephant, more fantastic and wild than any animal I had ever seen. And on the elephant's back stood a lady, beautiful and tall and strong as my mother herself had been beautiful and tall and strong.

My father came out of the woods behind me and dropped an armload of brush at the edge of the narrow road. "So there you are," he said. My horse cleared her throat noisily, happy to see my father, eager to return to work.

But I made no answer. Nor did I look up. In my mind I wandered far away with that grand circus elephant and beautiful circus lady.

My father walked over to me. Gently, he put his hand on my shoulder. "What's this? Dreaming again?" he asked.

Dreaming? I wondered. What was real and what was dreams?

Two years before, in the spring, when there were four of us in my family and we lived in the old log house and life flowed steadily along like the river that flows past our home to the sea—was that real, or was that nothing but a dream? Then, when the nightmare fire leapt up and stole my house, my baby sister, my mother away from me (and I and my father in the woods and too late to save our own family)—was that real, or a dream too horrible to be real? The dreams that some- times woke me in the dark of night (dreams of my mother coming back, of things being how they used to be)—were those not more real than anything that hap- pened in the light of day?

And this elephant and lady in a picture on a tree—
were they real? Could they march off the paper right
into my life? Could dreams become flesh? Could magic
live?

"What's it say, Pa? What's this paper doin' here?" I
asked, staring at the maze of words plastered all over
the poster.

"Hmm. Seems there's a circus coming, Son."

"Circus?"

"A 'Grand Menagerie' of animals. A 'Museum of
Wonders' from the 'Four Corners of the World.'"

"Coming *here*?"

"Next week. To Saint John."

"Really?" I asked. (I had never seen a circus before. I
had never seen an elephant before. Fact was, I had never
seen any animal larger than our oxen, or more exciting
than the black bear I saw once while hunting with my
pa.)

"Really," my father laughed.

"Well come on, Pa. Read it to me," I begged, as a
million questions raced through my mind. "When can
we go? How much does it cost? We will go, won't we,
Pa? What will that elephant and lady do in the circus
show?"

My father was much amused by my impatience. "A
circus, eh? An elephant coming to Saint John. Imagine
that!"

But instead of reading the poster, my pa reached out
and took it down from the tree. "Don't suppose
anybody else will see this way out here," he said, and he

folded the paper up and put it into his pocket.

"But Pa...?" I started to ask.

"Don't worry, Son—there'll be time to read it later. *After* we get our work done."

Chapter Two

That evening, I and my father sat on the stoop at the front of our partly finished house. By the light of the moon, we watched the Saint John River flow by.

Usually this was my favourite place for dreaming. Many times, when the day's work was done—when my father and I came home from hunting deer in the woods; fishing salmon in the streams; cutting firewood in the forest; planting and harvesting potatoes, vegetables and hay; minding the oxen, cows, chickens and sheep; bedding our horses down for the night—many times would we stand there and watch the graceful sailing ships and powerful new steamships come out from the harbour of Saint John.

How I loved to watch those ships race ahead of the wind, down the river by our farm, on their way out the mouth of the river and into the Bay of Fundy, past the shores of British North America and the United States, way off to the Atlantic Ocean and the great wide world beyond.

Though I had never been further from home than upriver to Saint John, many times in my mind had I travelled the seven seas in those ships that sailed past my door.

That evening, though, my mind did not sail away with ships.

"Read it to me again, Pa," I pleaded. "Please?"

If I could have read it all myself; if my mother had lived and continued to teach me; if I had not been needed on the farm and had a chance like rich city boys to become a scholar; let me assure you: I would have read that poster a hundred times or more that night!

Already my pa had read it to me twice, but still I wanted to know every detail of the circus that was coming to Saint John.

"Read what?" my father asked, teasing, as if he did not know what dreams filled my head.

"The circus poster," I said. "Read it to me, please."

"I don't know," my father said. "We have a big day ahead of us tomorrow. Hadn't we better get to bed?"

"One more time?" I begged.

And so, as the damp chill of night seeped into our bones, my father and I went into our house and sat by the flickering light of the fireplace. And for the third time that evening my father read:

FOR THREE DAYS ONLY

Great Attraction!
In Saint John, New Brunswick,
British North America
DEXTER'S LOCOMOTIVE WAX MUSEUM
and
BURGESS' MENAGERIE OF SERPENTS AND BIRDS
with its famous & splendid
Two-Ton Omnibus
*drawn by a team of **Six White Horses**
housing* PANORAMAS, PAINTINGS,
AND DIORAMAS &c. &c.

and
our world-famous MENAGERIE:
a rare collection of Animals *and* Birds
among these are the GNU, or horned horse,
LIONS, TIGERS, MONKEYS, CAMELS, HORSES, ZEBRA &c.
rare curiosities such as
Boa Constrictor and Anaconda
live serpents from the Island of Ceylon

and
the fantastic DEXTER AND BURGESS band
the **Drunken Soldier, Black Nights for Angeline,**
an original musical melodrama
MR. JESTIN, comic celebrity
*the beautiful SELENA, rider **extraordinaire***
&c. &c. &c. &c. &c.

AND
none other than
The Incomparable
Magnificent
Amazing
MOGUL

THE Mighty Elephant,

Wonder of the EAST

Largest Beast on the Face of the Earth
will be ridden by the Beautiful Selena

★

Performances will be:
★ Tues. October 18, Wed. October 19, Thurs. October 20 ★
each day at 10am and 2pm
★ Admission: Adults, 2s. 6d.; Children under 10, 1s. 3d. ★
Please note, good citizens of Saint John:
The Dexter and Burgess Circus will be:
arriving by land from Nova Scotia, Monday October 17
(or Tues. Oct. 18 depending on weather)
and
departing by sea on Saint John's own steamer
the ROYAL TAR
from Peter's Wharf on Fri. morning, Oct. 21, 1836

BE THERE ONE AND ALL!

"Imagine...an elephant coming to Saint John," my father said again when he finished reading the circus flyer. He stared into the fire.

I wondered—oh, I wondered—if there was any chance that Pa would take me to the circus show. He looked so old and tired sitting there, I remember thinking then. There never seemed to be time or money left over for fun anymore. Though we worked hard from morning until night, six days of the week the whole year through, still we were very poor. And since my mother had died in the fire, it seemed that Pa didn't really care for fun any longer.

Though I wanted with all my heart to go see the wonderful circus, I knew that I dared not pester Pa again to ask if we could go.

And so, I warmed my hands one last time over the glowing embers of the fire in our open fireplace. I bade my father good night, and pulled my heavy homespun shirt over my head and my socks from my feet and stood on the cold plank floor of our new and unfinished house. I pulled my trousers off and pulled my long, scratchy, wool nightshirt on over my head, and climbed the makeshift ladder to my homemade bunk. My body curled up small under the heavy blankets and I tried to sleep.

But as my father sat staring into the dying fire, and even later, as he snored heavily in his bed, I could not go to sleep. I could think only of the circus, the elephant, the lady—and of whether my pa and I could go to see the show.

Chapter Three

Next morning, I awoke to find Pa standing fully dressed at the side of my bed. He was shaking my shoulder. It was still dark out but I knew at once that I had overslept. Pa had already had his oatmeal porridge and a cup of tea, and was waiting for me to come help him with the chores.

"Sorry, Pa," I said, bolting up in my bed. I crawled out from under the warm blankets and jumped down from the bunk onto the freezing floor. I shivered and began to throw on my clothes.

Pa started for the door but then turned back to me. He reached into his pocket, pulled out the folded circus waybill, and put the special paper down on my bed. "By the way," he said, "I was thinking about that elephant."

"Yes," I said, staring at the folded poster. "Me too."

"I think we should go see that circus," he said softly.

"What?" I asked, looking up to my father. "Truly? Hurrah! Me too!"

A moment before I had been fast asleep, dreaming. Now I was wide awake and it seemed like the dream was coming true.

"Can we really go, Pa? Honest?" I asked as my father opened the door of our house.

"Sure enough. If we get our chores done," he said. He headed towards our rough log barn.

I felt like throwing my arms around my pa in a big

bear hug—like I used to do before I was eleven going on twelve. Instead, I just scrambled after him, pulling on my trousers and boots as I ran to catch up.

I couldn't believe it—we were really going to go see the circus and the elephant that was coming to Saint John!

Usually I was good with the animals. I was like my ma that way, Pa said many times. But that morning, I seemed to do everything wrong.

When I was letting our two oxen out of their pen in the barn, I got my hand caught in the gate, couldn't get out of the way, and nearly got my foot squashed by the heavy hoof of an ox. I accidentally spilled a half-pail of cold water on one of the sheep—and she wasn't happy at all. Worst of all, when I was reaching up to put a halter on my horse, she tossed her head back, and I slipped and fell right into a big mucky pile of manure.

Out of the corner of my eye, I caught my father smiling at me as he worked. I was embarrassed—and I was angry too.

"Had a hard night last night, did you?" my father asked in his teasing way.

I said nothing.

"Dreaming about the camels and snakes, were you?" he asked.

"No," I said angrily.

"Maybe it was Mr. Jestin, that clown, that you were dreaming about."

"I'm not a kid, Pa!"

"Was it the lions then? The monkeys? The zebra?"

I ignored his teasing and went back to scraping horse manure from the seat of my pants.

My father leaned against the side of the horse's stall. He was still smiling, but now there was no teasing in his voice. "It's going to be quite a show—that menagerie—eh, Son?"

I looked up at my father's face. I wondered what dreams had filled his head when he was a boy.

"What would you like to see more than anything else at that circus?" my pa asked, looking straight down into my eyes.

I tried to imagine what the unusual menagerie would be like.

"More than anything? I'd like to see the elephant," I confessed in a whisper. "Mogul and Selena. The elephant and his beautiful lady."

My father did not tease. "Hmm," he said. "Me too."

Everything was quiet in the barn then, quiet and warm and still. I climbed to the little loft and threw down some hay for the animals. How I loved the sweet sharp smell of hay!

For some reason, I thought of my mother, of her long brown hair and the kindness in her eyes. I wished so much she were there with Pa and me then.

Chapter Four

On Tuesday, October eighteenth, in the year of our Lord eighteen hundred and thirty-six, my father and I got up at four o'clock in the morning, just as we did any other day we were taking produce to town. We loaded our turnips on the oxcart the same as any other day we were going to market. We rattled our way over the dirt road through the woods exactly as we rattled any other time we went to Saint John.

But that morning I wasn't lulled to sleep by the clatter of the cart's heavy wheels on the rocks and hard-packed clay of the road. That morning I couldn't have slept if I had tried.

The circus would be in town—it said so on the poster, said it would be arriving the day before, on Monday— and my pa and I were going to see the first show before noon that very day!

As we crossed over a bridge and came to the frame buildings on the edge of Saint John, I noticed that other things were different that morning as well. I was not surprised to see people up and around so early in the day, but I was not sure why there were so many of them and why they were all lined up along both sides of Waterloo Street. It seemed to me that everyone was staring at me and my father, our two oxen and our slow, noisy cart full of vegetables as we clattered down the street.

Then, suddenly, the people along the street began to cheer. I was confused. Why would anyone whistle and clap for a poor farmer and his son and a cart full of turnips?

And then I heard a sound, a long high musical trumpeting sound that reverberated through my body, a powerful wild sound that made me tremble with excitement, a magical sound that would change my life forever.

I turned around on the rough seat of the cart to see what the sound could be.

The crowd cheered. The trumpeting shot through me once again. I shivered, full of wonder and fear.

There behind me, marching over the crest of the hill, as if it were bursting out of the paper poster I had seen on the pine tree, as if it were coming to life in one of my dreams, was a marvellous circus parade.

And leading the parade was none other than the "incomparable, magnificent, amazing Mogul, the Mighty Elephant, the Wonder of the East, the Largest Beast on the Face of the Earth."

"It's Mogul, Pa. It's the elephant!" I shouted with delight.

"I dare say it is," my father replied, taking a quick look over his shoulder at the circus parade. "Imagine!"

"They didn't arrive yesterday, after all!"

My father promptly pulled the oxen to the side of the road, out of the way of the parade, and stopped the cart just in time for the parade to pass by us. I could practically reach out and touch it.

First came Mogul, a saddle—all blue and gold and silver—on his back. He was enormous, this elephant, with a huge, leathery, almost hairless body and a massive head. Wild and powerful and majestic as a king, he rhythmically planted one heavy foot at a time on the dirt street. Between his two white tusks—one shorter than the other—his long trunk swayed effortlessly back and forth.

On Mogul's high saddle sat Selena. Her dress was short and ruffled, and as white as the snow that soon would blanket our New Brunswick woods. Her jewels of diamonds and gold sparkled in the sun. Her blonde hair—long like my mother's brown hair—streamed out behind her in the breeze. Like my mother, Selena was tall and slender. Like my mother, she was strong.

Selena's long legs held tight to the elephant and she stretched out her arms to all in the crowd. But though Selena smiled and waved at everyone, it seemed to me that, for one moment in time, she looked straight down into my eyes with a warm smile that was for me alone.

"It's Selena," was all I could say.

"I dare say it is," was all that my father replied.

Behind Mogul and Selena, six white horses pulled a huge circus omnibus painted every colour of the rainbow. High up on the seat at the front of this wagon stood a tall, dignified man—taller even than my father. I thought he must be the leader of the circus, the master, and he wore a long black coat and a tall black hat and he watched his parade as if he were the general of some magnificent marching army.

On the roof of the omnibus—it made me laugh to see it—a wiry little man dressed in a bright blue shirt with puffed sleeves kept trying to stand on his head and his hands. Each time his upside-down body pointed straight up in the air, he would fall onto the flat top of the wagon.

Once he turned his clumsy fall into a smart somersault across the wagon, dangerously close to its edge. Once he sharply cartwheeled along the length of the wagon. And once he pretended to fall off the back edge of the wagon—only to grab on to a railing and hang suspended over the end of the jostling omnibus.

Behind the omnibus came a parade of the strangest carts I had ever seen. They were all painted bright colours. Their wheels were tall, their reins and rigging were long, and those carts rumbled down Waterloo Street past us.

On the first cart, the circus band played loud, brassy music that pierced the cool fall air. The music was like the elephant's call: wild, wonderful, foreign and free. It sent shivers of excitement up my spine.

The rest of the carts hauling this menagerie and museum on the country roads from town to town (all the way from Massachusetts to Maine, Maine to Nova Scotia, Nova Scotia to here, New Brunswick) carried the cages of all the amazing animals and birds of the DEXTER AND BURGESS caravan...pelicans and parrots and fancy golden pheasants; comical monkeys and hyenas; powerful lions and tigers; scary snakes—a boa constrictor and an anaconda; camels and wonderful-looking horses and a black-and-white striped zebra; and a strange-looking creature that looked like it was half-ox, half-horse.

I stood on tiptoe on the seat of our little cart. I could not get enough of this magic circus parade. It was going by us so fast. It was like a dream to me, like a dream come true, the kind of dream I never wanted to end.

But the last of the parade did pass us by. The last carts of animals rolled past us, rolled on down the road.

Behind them, the city boys (those carefree boys from Saint John that I saw—but never got to know—each time I came to market) were racing after the circus parade, running to see the circus set up its pavilion tents.

"I guess we'd better get over to King Street and down to Market Square to sell these vegetables now," my pa said, breaking into my silence.

Sadly I turned from the colourful circus world of dreams to the everyday world of Pa, the oxen and the mound of turnips in our ramshackle cart.

"I suppose so," I replied, sitting down and trying not to watch the other boys run down Waterloo Street into the heart of Saint John.

"Of course, if you'd rather go see the circus set up, I don't imagine things will be too busy for me to handle alone," my pa added.

I looked into my father's eyes. Did he really know me so well? Did he understand what I wanted so badly? Could I really go with the other boys and see the circus set up its show?

"Well, don't hang around thinking about it," he said cheerfully, "you don't want to miss anything!"

And so I jumped down from the cart and raced gaily down Waterloo Street after the other boys and the circus parade.

I never ran so fast in my life.

Chapter Five

Down Waterloo Street, around the corner and down Union Street, down to the corner of Union and Charlotte streets, the other boys and I ran.

Around the edges of a huge green field, all the carts in the circus parade had pulled up. Already everyone was exploding into action.

How could they get everything ready in time for a show that morning? I wondered.

We boys got as close to the DEXTER AND BURGESS Caravan as we could without getting scolded by the busy circus people. Some of us sat and leaned along a hitching post at one corner of the field and watched while the circus began to set up its three large white canvas pavilions.

Each human and animal member of the DEXTER AND BURGESS troupe worked like part of a great machine, pulling up the canvas tents. The horses and camels, the zebra and gnu, all helped, moving the heavy centre poles into place, and pulling on the thick ropes to set the canvas tents up. Then the people of the troupe scrambled everywhere at once, pulling smaller ropes out to stretch the canvas tight, putting short poles all around the outside of the tent.

Mogul, the biggest and strongest of them all, pushed with his head, pulled with the colossal muscles of his body and lifted with his trunk, helping to get the great pavilions ready for the morning show. Beside the elephant walked his trainer. The stout, elderly, bearded man guided Mogul with firm, gentle orders.

"I imagine I could get Mogul working faster than that old guy," a city boy with a grey cap boasted to me.

"You could?" I asked.

"Sure. I'd just whip him a little and then he'd listen to me all right."

I looked at the great elephant, noble and proud. How could anyone be cruel to such a magnificent creature? How could this boy from Saint John even consider it?

"Aw, you're full of pig manure," said another city boy. He was sitting on the top rail of the fence next to me, wearing a fancy store-bought suit and tie. "What do you know about elephants anyway? You've never been close to an elephant and you never will be any closer to one than you are right now!"

"Oh yeah? Well as a matter of fact, I'll probably be riding that elephant before this week is out," the boy with the grey cap bragged.

The boy in the suit just laughed.

"Do you really mean that?" I asked. (I couldn't believe that any boy would be allowed to ride Mogul.)

"I guess I do mean it," the boy with the grey cap cockily told all of us. "For your information, all the people belonging to this here Menagerie are going to be staying at my ma's hotel. You see that man there?" He pointed to the man from the circus omnibus, the tall one with the long black coat. "That's Mr. H. H. Fuller. He's the master of this circus troupe. I'm here to give him a message from my ma. Why I'll bet he gives me free tickets to come to the circus every day!"

"Who cares if he does?" asked the boy in the fancy clothes. "My father is buying me tickets for all six shows anyway."

"Yeah, but I'll bet Mr. H. H. Fuller lets me ride Mogul," the boy in the grey cap continued.

"That's nothing," said the fancy boy. "My father's taking me to Peter's Wharf to see the circus board the *Royal Tar* on Friday."

"Well, just between you and me," the boy in the grey cap whispered confidentially, "I wouldn't be surprised if Mr. H. H. Fuller invites me to join up with this circus. I just might be with them when that steamer leaves come Friday."

"I don't believe you," laughed the other boy.

"Are you really joining the circus?" I asked the boy in the grey cap, not sure whether he was making up stories or not.

"You bet," he replied. "They need lots of boys to run this show."

"Don't worry about him," the fancy boy said to me. "He ain't old enough to join no circus anyhow."

"Oh yeah?" the boy in the grey cap answered. "I'm twelve years old—that's plenty old to be a circus boy! There's Mr. Fuller now. I think I'll go talk to him right away," he said importantly. "Mr. Fuller! Mr. Fuller!" he called, running after the circus master.

"I don't believe him," the other boy said to me scornfully. But I could tell by the way he watched Mr. Fuller and the boy talking that he, like me, really envied the boastful boy in the grey cap.

And I envied both the city boys. How I would love to see all of the circus shows. How I would love to see the circus board the *Royal Tar* at Peter's Wharf come Friday. How I would love to ride Mogul, the elephant.

And how, more than anything else in the whole wonderful world, I would love to join the circus and travel with it to far-off places on the steamship *Royal Tar*.

Chapter Six

Going to DEXTER'S LOCOMOTIVE WAX MUSEUM AND BURGESS' MENAGERIE OF SERPENTS AND BIRDS with my father that morning was even better than my fantasies about it. Life *was* magic, with my nose full of the smells of roasting chestnuts and piping hot popcorn all covered with butter; my ears full of the noises of so many people and of the strange animals from all over the world; my eyes full of the colours and strange sights of the DEXTER AND BURGESS circus.

My pa bought a piece of liquorice for himself and a sugar candy for me and we stood in a long line of people waiting to get into the omnibus. From the outside the omnibus was just a big square box of a wagon. But inside it was a room full of marvellous displays.

There were paintings of famous events—like the one on the death of Napoleon. There were dioramas, models that showed real disasters that had happened in our world.

Even though people were crowding all around me in the omnibus, I stood still and stared transfixed at the scene of *The Conflagration of New York*. How terrible to see the murderous fire racing through the city, completely out of control! How horrible to see people fleeing in every direction! How awful it must have been for Ma and my baby sister! How could anything under God's Heaven be as dreadful as the destruction of fire?

"Come now, Son," my father was saying. His hand felt good on my shoulder. "Let's go see the rest of the exhibition."

Outside the entrance to the first pavilion I saw a young girl with a grey bag over her shoulder. She was holding up one of the circus waybills for everyone to see. I looked at her shyly, even smiled a bit, but something was very peculiar about her. She was staring straight ahead and did not blink or move in any way at all.

I wanted to ask Pa what was wrong with her, but my father was tugging on my hand, pulling me into the tent.

Once inside the great pavilion, Pa and I both stopped dead in our tracks, even though the crowd in the line behind us was pushing to get inside. Behind rope barriers were many people inside the tent standing perfectly still—just like the girl outside the tent. The diffused bright sunlight of the tent gave an unearthly glow to these strange figures, dressed in unusual clothes from long-ago times and from all over the world.

To my surprise, my father suddenly laughed. None of the figures moved at all. Pa explained it to me, smiling to himself all the while. The people behind the ropes—and the girl I had seen—weren't alive at all, Pa said. They were wax statues.

I wasn't quite sure whether to believe Pa or not. People of wax could not be real, I knew, yet they looked as real as you or me, so real it was eerie...Moses in the

Bulrushes; a one-eyed monster called the Cyclops; Cleopatra; Alexander the Great; some wise man named Socrates; Julius Caesar; the mighty Hercules; the brave Robin Hood; General George Washington ("the first President of the United States of America, taken from a bust executed from Life, in 1786," my father read to me); and even the King of England and British North America, King William IV. ("They call him King William, the 'Sailor King', the 'Royal Tar'," my father told me. "Commander Reed's steamship, the *Royal Tar*, is named after him.")

I peered into the eyes of each of the statues to see if they would blink. I kept peeking behind me at them to see if they were moving or breathing. I couldn't quite believe that these lifelike figures weren't real.

But if the paintings and panoramas of the world's disasters and the wax statues of exotic people were wonderful to me, the animals in the Menagerie in the second pavilion were *absolutely amazing*.

Excitedly I ran from cage to cage, thrilled to see these unusual creatures "from the four corners of the world," calling to my father to catch up, marvelling that each cage held something more fantastic than the last.

There were the peculiar birds—pheasants and funny-looking pelicans and parrots that talked—birds so much more beautiful and exciting than the ordinary chickens, ducks, crows, gulls, sparrows and chickadees I was used to at home.

There were the gigantic boa constrictor and anaconda—great snakes from Ceylon—grander and deadlier than the humble water snakes and garter snakes I liked to watch and play with on my farm.

There were the ferocious lions and tigers from Africa and India—with growls wilder and more powerful than any animal that hid in the shadows of my New Brunswick woods.

The playful monkeys looked like they would be even more fun to play with than the puppy I had when I was young.

Even the large gentle animals that reminded me of my horse—the camels, a striped zebra, a horned gnu—were more colourful, more unusual, more intriguing, more magic than the horse I loved so much back at home.

Yet at the same time these animals were strange—ever so strange—they also seemed familiar and comfortable to me.

The gnu had come from halfway around the world, from Africa, to my New Brunswick home. His head and horns looked like those of our ox, his mane and tail were like those of my horse, and his body was like the deer we hunted in the woods. But as I talked to that animal, as I threw him a piece of carrot I was eating, I realized that this strange creature, this *wildebeest*, was really not that much different than my horse at home.

This gnu ate food like my horse. He made manure like my horse—and circus boys not much older than me cleaned it up just as I cleaned up after my horse. This gnu breathed deeply and stood solidly and slept standing up and stared at me with intelligent brown eyes—just as my horse did.

But what about the elephant? I wondered. Could you talk to an elephant, pet him, feed him, take care of him, love him, the way I loved my horse? Or was the elephant too wild and dangerous—did you need to whip him and scare him like the city boy said?

Chapter Seven

I could have spent all day just watching and talking to the animals. But before long, the circus band struck up a fanfare to announce the first performance of the DEXTER AND BURGESS troupe.

"Walk up! Walk right up! Step up here, ladies and gentlemen, boys and girls!" Mr. H. H. Fuller called out in his booming voice from the door of the final and largest tent. "Step up! Come in! Gather round! Find yourselves a seat, one and all, good citizens of Saint John!"

My father and I bustled with the rest of the crowd through the flap door of the tent, and towards rough wooden benches that had been built around a huge sawdust ring in the centre of the pavilion.

"Walk up! Walk up!" the circus master shouted over the hubbub as he walked into the tent and to the centre of the ring. "Let us entertain you with tricks and jokes and songs and plays and feats of daring never before witnessed here!"

The benches were filling up quickly. Circus master Fuller was hurrying everybody along. I had never seen so many people in one place at one time.

"Saint John must be the biggest city in the whole world," I said to my pa as we edged our way to a place we had spotted in the fourth row.

"Oh no," he told me, "there are even bigger cities

across the ocean in Europe and down in the Boston States."

I sat down, wedged on the rough bench between my pa and a young woman who smiled kindly at me. I sat as tall as I could to see past the hat on the lady in front of me—nothing was going to stop me from seeing any part of this special show.

First, Mr. Jestin sang a comical song. I didn't understand most of it, but as I felt my father laughing beside me (how long it had been since he had laughed as much as he had this day), and as I felt the woman beside me and all the people in the circus pavilion laughing as if they were all one person, then I laughed too.

If you had asked me to explain what was so funny, I couldn't have done it. It didn't matter anymore what was funny, only that everyone was laughing together.

Then four white horses—bare-backed, red ribbons tied in their manes and tails—were led into the ring by circus boys. The horses cantered around and around the outside of the performance circle.

Suddenly, Selena and a circus man cartwheeled in between some of the horses, into the centre of the ring. Trumpets blared and the two performers vaulted onto the backs of two horses at exactly the same time.

The two riders gained their balance, then stood up perfectly straight, riding the backs of the quickly moving horses, their knees and ankles flexing automatically as if they had become a part of the horses themselves. The circus man stood on his hands on his horse's back while Selena stood on her horse's back juggling three balls that a circus boy had thrown to her.

Finally, two circus boys ran in with large hoops on the ends of sticks; they held the hoops high above the backs of the horses. At exactly the same time, Selena and the circus man whirled around on the backs of their horses, leapt high in the air through the hoops and landed on the backs of the horses that galloped behind them.

I must have forgotten to breathe during that part of the show, so excited was I about the daring display of horsemanship. Indeed, as Selena and the circus man somersaulted from the backs of the horses to land gracefully on the sawdust floor of the ring, all of us in the audience let out a giant sigh and cheered as if sharing one voice.

Then something unusual and disturbing occurred. Selena and the circus man, the circus boys, and three of the horses all left the pavilion ring. One horse kept galloping around the ring. A fat man dressed like a soldier staggered out of the audience and stumbled into the circus ring—right in front of the charging white horse.

The horse had to stop dead in his tracks, going up on his hind legs to keep from crushing the man. The man didn't seem to notice the horse at all. The horse came down on all fours right by the man, and snorted to get the man's attention. The man hiccoughed loudly, unaware that he had left the audience for the circus ring.

"Oh no," my father whispered to me. "He's drunk." When the man finally noticed the white circus horse in front of him, he weaved drunkenly back and forth as he walked to the horse's side. He tried to hoist himself up on the horse's back, but he fell back down into the sawdust.

For a moment I thought the face under the too-big soldier's hat looked familiar. People in the audience were whispering to each other about who this man could be and what he was doing there interrupting the circus show and endangering his life.

The man threw himself up on the horse again, only this time he slid right over the other side of the horse and landed hard again on the ground.

A few people in the audience laughed.

The man tried one last time to get on the horse's back. This time he succeeded in getting up, but when he sat up he was facing the back of the horse. Immediately the horse began to trot, then canter, then gallop around the ring.

Dangerously the man jostled backwards and forwards and side to side as if he would fall off at any moment. Then he leaned ahead and reached out for where he thought the horse's head should be.

I laughed when the fat drunken soldier lifted up the horse's tail looking for the horse's head.

When he couldn't find the head, the soldier stood up on the back of the horse, lurching around in his inebriation, still looking for the right end of the horse.

"Sit down! Don't do it! Be careful!" yelled voices from the crowd.

But the man kept standing up, somehow managing

to stay balanced on the back of the galloping horse. First the man looked back, then clumsily jumped around to face the other way, where he found the front end of the horse. As soon as he saw it, he dove through the air towards the neck of the horse.

All of us in the audience stopped laughing and gasped, thinking he was going to fall to the ground right under the pounding hoofs of the horse. My father gripped my hand.

But—wonder of wonders—at the last possible moment, the man threw his arms around the neck of the horse and hung there, dangling from the horse's neck, facing the horse, being carried—almost dragged— backwards quickly around the ring.

The intoxicated soldier vaulted suddenly up onto the back of the horse again. How could he do this in his state? I wondered. What prevented him from falling off?

Tipsily he stood on the back of the galloping horse once more. He wiped sweat from his brow, then started to take off his jacket and his pants. Why didn't he fall to the ground? He threw his jacket into the audience. Then he threw off his trousers.

Under his jacket was another jacket, and under that a sweater, and then shirt after shirt after shirt—and the fat man took them all off except his underwear. Under his trousers were pair after pair of pants—and he took them all off while the horse galloped steadily around the ring.

And suddenly I realized that this peculiar man was neither fat nor drunk nor a soldier nor even a member of the audience at all. He took off his oversized soldier's hat, tossed it into the crowd, smartly threw his arms out at his side, and did a flip from the horse to land on his feet on the ground. It was none other than Mr. Jestin himself!

I, and everyone in the audience, laughed. We laughed with relief that the drunken soldier had not been pounded to a pulp by the hoofs of the horse, laughed that Mr. Jestin was so clever and agile, laughed most of all because we had been fooled by the circus performer.

I would not be so easily fooled by the next act. At least I did not think I would.

Chapter Eight

The circus troupe performed a melodrama then, the first play that I had ever seen. In my mind, I knew well enough that under the costumes and make-up the characters of the play were really Mr. Fuller, Mr. Jestin, Selena and the other circus performers. Still, something about the music, the fancy costumes and the exciting story pulled me into the drama of that little play—until the fantasy on stage became quite real to me.

Selena played the part of Angeline Arabella, a virtuous young woman about to be married. Mr. Fuller was her rich stepfather and—for some reason I did not understand—he was insisting that she marry Mr. Balfour Black, a rich newcomer to the village.

In every other part of the circus show Mr. Jestin had made me laugh. But from the moment he came on stage as Balfour Black, he sent shivers of fear through me. Except for a frilly white shirt, Mr. Jestin was dressed all in pitch-black clothes. His face was ghostly white, with red lips, bushy black eyebrows and a huge black moustache. When he grabbed Selena by the wrist and forced her to the floor and said, "You will do *prrrecisely* what I say, and you *will marrrrry* me!", I knew that Balfour Black was unredeemably evil and definitely not the man for Angeline.

The radiant Angeline, of course, did not love the wicked Balfour Black. She loved Fred Fergus, a poor,

honest farmhand played by one of the older circus boys.

When the evil Mr. Black kidnapped Angeline and locked her in a room and went off to plan how to steal her money and kill her, I was furious at his despicable behaviour.

And when Selena—all alone in that room without help—began to sing about all her problems, my throat choked up with tears.

Where was Fred Fergus? I worried. I wanted to barge into that room, and untie Angeline, and carry her away to....

How thrilled I was when Fred Fergus did just that—just what I would do! Strong, tall, manly Fred Fergus burst through the door of the stage house. Quickly he untied Angeline. He checked that she was all right, then took her out the door to safety.

Angeline, so grateful and so happy to be alive, stopped Fred, leaned up and kissed the hero on the cheek. (How I envied Fred just then.)

But just at that moment when everything seemed perfect, who should arrive—riding a real horse right onto the stage—but...?

Forgetting where I was and that this was only a play, I called out to warn Angeline. I couldn't help it—I shouted out loud. But instead of saying "Angeline," I shouted, "Watch out, *Selena*! It's Mr. Black!"

When I realized what I had done, I was afraid that everybody would laugh at me. I looked around. Strangely enough, nobody seemed to mind. In fact, everybody in the audience was busy hissing and booing the evil man.

And everything turned out fine in the story after that anyway. Fred Fergus fought Balfour Black, and Angeline's stepfather found out that Black was really a villain, and some woman from the village came forward and proved that Fred was really the orphan son of a rich businessman who had left him piles and piles of money, and Fred and Angeline got married to live happily ever after!

And my pa and the woman beside me and the people of Saint John and I all cheered, and some of us felt tears trickle down our cheeks, so moved were we to see good triumph over evil and to see the beautiful Angeline in the strong arms of Fred Fergus while the wicked Mr. Black ran headlong off into the night.

Full of joy and excitement, I could not imagine anything more wonderful than the fantastic things I had seen that day.

But then, more awesome than the tragic story of Angeline; the model of the terrible fire in New York; the almost-alive statues of wax; the animals at once strange and familiar; the funny songs of Mr. Jestin; the horse-back-riding; more wonderful than all these wonders put together; better than any picture on any poster on any tree; bigger and more thrilling than in the circus parade; more exciting than anything I had ever seen; better even than my dreams about this day—Mogul entered the ring, Selena walking at his side.

The elephant was massive, stately, full of power, a huge wild animal from the jungles of India. My eyes were open wide. My mouth was too. How could any living creature be so gigantic and so strong?

Next to the grey leathery bulk of the elephant, the lady Selena looked delicate and white, tall and thin, beautiful and strong.

"Walk, Mogul," Selena commanded in a voice that was gentle and private, yet strong and firm enough to reach my ears. The elephant marched, one huge round foot at a time, around the ring. The band played a fanfare and the crowd and I applauded.

"Turn, Mogul," Selena commanded, and the gigantic elephant turned in a tight circle on the spot. The band played and the crowd cheered at his agility.

Mr. Jestin walked through the ring, dressed in old, baggy clothes. Out of one big pocket flopped a giant handkerchief. Out of the other stood a corked water bottle. In his hand was a big red apple.

Mogul deftly reached out his trunk and pulled the handkerchief out of Mr. Jestin's pocket. He carefully placed the handkerchief on Mr. Jestin's head.

"Stop that, you brute!" Mr. Jestin said, pretending to be angry. Everyone in the audience laughed.

Mr. Jestin put the apple in his mouth, turned his back on Mogul, and started to walk away. Mogul swung out his trunk again. Dextrously he snatched the apple from Mr. Jestin's lips, carried it back and dropped it in his own cavernous mouth, and crushed the whole thing in a strong bite with his four giant teeth.

Mr. Jestin protested once again, while my father and I and everyone in the crowd clapped for Mogul's cleverness and laughed at his mischief.

Finally Mr. Jestin turned to walk away once more. Mogul reached out his trunk and—you must believe me, for I saw it with my own eyes—took the cork from the bottle, dropped the cork to the ground, picked up the bottle and carried it up and back to his mouth, and poured the water down his throat. All without spilling a drop of water from the bottle!

Apparently, Mr. Jestin didn't even know Mogul had touched the bottle! Everyone in the audience was cheering and whistling and calling out to Mr. Jestin. But it was Mogul who walked over to the surprised man and gave him back his empty water bottle.

The people in the giant white pavilion were all clapping their hands, rhythmically applauding the clever elephant.

"Foot out, Mogul," Selena then ordered softly. For a moment the elephant hesitated, refused to budge, stared into Selena's eyes. For one instant I thought that Mogul might not obey the command. Why should this six thousand pound beast listen to the woman who stood below him? He had the strength of forty humans; why should he obey just one?

"Foot out, Mogul," Selena repeated. Her voice was firm. She showed no weakness in front of the elephant. But neither did she show hatred or disrespect for the mighty animal.

The elephant put his big right foot out in front of him.

Selena lightly stood up on the foot. "Trunk down," Selena firmly commanded. The elephant looked her in the eye, then put his trunk down as if he were a gentleman bowing before a queen. Selena stepped onto his trunk.

"Trunk up, Mogul," Selena ordered and, as I and the crowd held our breath, the powerful elephant lifted the circus lady standing on his trunk up, up, high off the ground. Holding her balanced with the end of his trunk, he gently but surely set her down on his back. The band played and we all cheered even more.

"Feet up, Mogul," Selena said, and up went first one of the elephant's mighty front feet, then the other, onto a small painted box. The band played and Mogul's great back feet moved to the music around the box and it seemed that my father and the woman beside me and all the people of Saint John were whistling and stamping their feet and clapping and roaring their congratulations.

And I was cheering loudest of all. Looking across the ring, I stared straight into the small eyes in the mammoth head of the great beast. The elephant *was* powerful and wild, I thought, but the elephant might also be gentle and wise.

With all my heart, I wished that elephant could be my friend.

Chapter Nine

P a, Pa! It was wonderful!" I exclaimed as we burst out of the circus tent into the bright glare of noon. "Can we come again this afternoon? Please!"

I wanted to dance and jump and hug him all at once.

"It certainly was a good show, wasn't it?" my father said. He squeezed his way through the crowd of people and bought me a glass of lemonade from a circus boy about my age. (How lucky that unsmiling boy was to travel around as part of this circus, I remember thinking as I watched him fill my glass.)

"Good? It was the most fantastic thing I ever did see," I said to my pa. "Please, can we see this afternoon's show too?"

"I'm glad you had fun," said my father.

My heart sank. All of a sudden, I realized that he was going to say no.

"This afternoon we've got chores to do at home."

He wasn't going to let me come back to the circus. "Tomorrow then, Pa? Or Thursday?" I asked. I couldn't imagine not seeing this circus once again.

"We've got firewood to cut for the winter, Son. You don't want to be cold, do you?"

"No, Pa, but...." Tears rose up in my throat. My joy was plunging into disappointment, and I did not want it so. I tried to fight it, but sadness was welling up inside me.

"There are more turnips to dig," my father chastised. "You don't want to go hungry, do you, Son?"

"But Pa...."

"There's the house to finish too. If...," My father stopped speaking. Sadness filled his eyes too.

"Listen," he spoke—impatiently for some reason I did not then fully understand—"we have plenty of work to do before winter. It costs money to go to the circus, money to see each part of the show, money that we can't spare. I brought you here today, didn't I?"

I did not answer my father. I was sorry to ask for more than he could give. But I so wanted to see the circus again.

"Let's not spoil the fun we had today. We had a good time today, didn't we, Son?"

Still I did not reply. I looked back at the huge white canvas pavilions. Was this the last I would see of the circus?

"I'm sorry, Son. That's just the way things are," my father said. And then my father turned from me and began to walk away from the circus grounds.

I did not want to follow him then. I wanted instead to stay at the circus and see another show.

My father walked without turning back to me. He expected me to follow, I knew, but I stayed rooted to my spot, halfway between him and the circus. Each step he took away from me, each step pulled at my heart. Did he not understand how much I wanted to stay? The more he walked away from me the more alone I felt, torn as I was between him and the DEXTER-BURGESS

MENAGERIE.

Then I saw Mogul come out of the circus tent with his old trainer. I saw the lemonade boy throw Mogul some peanuts from his stand. I saw the elephant's long trunk reach down and, as careful as the fingers on a hand, pick up one peanut at a time from the ground, and lift each to his mouth.

But that was all I saw. For tears blurred my vision and I turned and ran away from the elephant, away from the circus and after the small figure of my father walking to our oxcart.

Our cart bumped its way along the road in and out of the woods and down along the river towards our farm. My father and I did not speak the whole way home.

In fact, we did not speak much at all the next two days. During chores that night, my father tried to make conversation about the circus show.

"What was your favourite part of the circus?" he asked me.

"I beg your pardon, Sir?" I said, looking up from milking our cow.

"What did you like best at the circus? The snakes?"

I did not feel like playing games. "The elephant was my favourite part," I said softly.

"Oh. You liked Mogul," my father said.

"Yes," I said.

"And Selena?" my father asked.

"Yes," I replied and went back to the milking.

"Hmm. Me too."

And so it was for the next two long days, my father

and I working side by side, and me trying to return to a time before the circus, to a daily routine of him and me and work. Only now we did not speak with one another.

And the more I tried not to think of the circus, the more that elephant marched around in my thoughts.

Then came Thursday evening. Chores were done. My father leaned his hayfork carefully by the door of the barn—as I had seen him do so many times before—and prepared to go back to the house.

The circus would be leaving next morning.

I picked up a brush and, without speaking, brushed the flanks of my horse. I felt my father's eyes watch me, then heard the barn door close behind him. He would be walking alone now, back to the house.

I waited a few minutes for him to get settled in the house. I saddled up my horse. Then, even though night would soon be upon us, I quietly led her out of the barn and walked her up our lane.

Out of sight of the house, I climbed on my horse's back, clenched the reins, whispered "Giddyap!" in her ear, dug my heels into her side, and galloped full-speed up the lane towards the road.

At the top of the lane, my horse out of habit turned to go back to the barn, but I checked her with the reins. "Come on, girl, giddyap!" I said and raced down the road towards Saint John.

I could run away right then, I knew, as I galloped through the dark woods. I could run away and join the

DEXTER AND BURGESS circus. I could be on the *Royal Tar* the very next day, heading to large and wonderful cities, the United States of America, the whole amazing world that lay beyond the mouth of the Saint John River.

As I pounded along towards Saint John, the circus, Peter's Wharf and the *Royal Tar*, I thought of the city boys in their grey caps and fancy suits. How I envied them. How I wanted to do the things they talked about.

But, though I tried to put them out of my mind, I could not help but also think of my pa and my home—both of them getting further and further behind me as I rode.

At the top of a ridge, halfway between my home and Saint John, I suddenly pulled back hard on the reins. "Whoa, girl," I commanded my horse. She stopped and stood still, breathing in long, deep breaths.

From that height of land, I could look for miles in every direction. Towards Saint John, the red sun was setting in the trees. Back towards home, night's blackness was already settling in.

I was not afraid here, miles from any other human being—this was my home. But something tore at my heart.

As the sun's fire disappeared from the ashy grey sky, I thought of my father, sitting all alone by the fireplace. I remembered other times, times that now seemed as if in an uncertain dream, times when four of us sat by the hearth...me, my sister, my pa and the woman, my mother, I tried so hard to imagine now. I thought of the old log house in the woods on the bank of the Saint John River—the house that had been my home and then had burned. I thought of the new house, the home that my father was trying to make for the two of us now.

As I and my horse stood there on the ridge, I was torn between two feelings, equally strong, that tugged my heart in opposite directions. The feelings were like heavy ropes pulling hard at me; the feelings threatened to tear me in half. On one side pulled the oxen, the unfinished log house, the land, my horse and my pa; on the other pulled an elephant, a ship, the sea and a woman so like the mother I had lost in the fire.

What could I do?

I leaned forward. I buried my head in my horse's mane. My horse felt warm. I listened to deep steady breathing, not sure what was the horse's and what was my own. I stroked my horse's side with my hands. Trying to hold back my tears, I whispered to my horse, "What do you think, eh?"

My horse neighed softly, tossing her head, but she did not try to go ahead, nor did she turn to go home. It was getting dark and cold now; the first snows of winter would soon be here.

I hugged close to my horse and soaked in her warmth. And finally I whispered in her ear: "Haw." My horse turned gladly. "Home, girl," I said. My horse and I galloped through the night, galloped back to my home.

Chapter Ten

My father asked me no questions when I came in from my evening ride. He asked me nothing before I went to bed. He did not ask me anything next morning during chores.

I worked hard. I did not feel like talking. All I knew was that I must try very hard to get used to the fact that I would *never* see the circus, the elephant or Selena again. That very day I would not see them board the *Royal Tar* at Peter's Wharf in Saint John.

"Lots to do today," my father said when we finished our milking.

"Yes, Sir," I agreed.

"The last turnips to dig."

"Yes," said I.

"Still more firewood to cut."

"Yes."

My father stopped what he was doing. "Listen, Son, I think I understand what's upsetting you."

I said nothing. Could he really understand how I felt?

"It's hard to think of that circus leaving Saint John without seeing it again, isn't it?"

I nodded.

"You know that I'd like to see it again too, don't you?

He wanted to see it too? "Then why don't we?"

My father looked at me, long and hard. He smiled

and shook his head.

"We could take the two horses, Pa!"

"Yes, but...."

"If we hurried, we could catch the circus before it leaves Peter's Wharf!"

"Well...."

"That wouldn't cost us anything, Pa!"

"No, I guess it wouldn't." He smiled again.

"Please, can't we go?" I asked, hardly daring to gather up my shattered hopes.

"Why not, Son? Why not, indeed?" Pa finally said. "Here! Take these." Pa threw me a couple of apples to stuff in my jacket pocket. "Well, don't just stand there gawking. Get your horse ready! You don't want to miss it, do you? Hurry along now!"

How incredible! I could see the elephant one last time before the circus left! And Pa wanted to see him too. For once, I had to scurry to keep up with my father.

I have always loved to ride. But that day—Pa and I racing together along the road to Saint John—was surely one of the best. Pa's horse knew him and mine knew me and we all knew the road and it was one of those bracing fall mornings when the air is cold and clear as ice but the sun slices through the stone-cold world with the brilliance of fire.

As we neared Saint John, we soon found out that we weren't the only ones anxious to catch a last glimpse of the circus before it left for its home in America. People from all around the city were crowding into Saint John to bid the circus farewell.

From Duke Street to Market Square, all along the waterfront, people were thronging to see the circus one last time.

We had to tie our horses to a hitching rail several blocks away from the harbour. Then, with effort, we worked our way through the thousands of people converging on the wharves around Peter's Wharf. *Everyone* wanted to see DEXTER'S LOCOMOTIVE WAX MUSEUM AND BURGESS' MENAGERIE OF SERPENTS AND BIRDS board Saint John's brand-new sidewheeler steamer, the *Royal Tar*.

By the time we got anywhere close to the ship, we could see that the steamer was already crowded almost to bursting with the paraphernalia of the circus.

The fancy circus omnibus was already on board, up on the main deck towards the bow, just behind the steamboat's two tall smokestacks. How strange it seemed that this colourful wagon—with the other gaudy circus wagons—that had helped carry the circus hundreds of miles from cities in the Boston States to Halifax and smaller towns in Nova Scotia, then to towns and finally Saint John in New Brunswick, was now about to return to its home on the deck of a steamship sailing down the Atlantic coast.

From talking to people who had been watching since early morning, my father found out that the pelicans and parrots, golden pheasants, monkeys and hyenas, lions and tigers, boa constrictor and anaconda, were already safely locked in their cages below the decks.

We could see a huge stack of hay and barrels of water piled on the deck towards the stern of the ship, ready to feed the circus animals. Already cords of wood had been thrown below, ready to burn in the firebox, to make steam in the boilers, to drive the engines, to turn the huge wooden paddlewheels, to push the *Royal Tar* and her strange cargo through the ocean waters.

Poorly clothed people (new immigrants from Ireland, most likely) and rich cabin passengers already lined the ship's rails, anxious to set sail for Portland, Maine.

Only the large animals weren't yet on board.

To get a closer look at the ship and circus, I slipped away from my father. Being smaller and quicker than the adults, I inched my way closer to the ramp that had been set up to get the large animals from Peter's Wharf to the ship. In fact, by walking right on top of the huge timber that made a raised side for the wharf—being careful not to fall off into the water—I squeezed right up to the edge of the ramp itself.

Looking one way down the ramp, I had a good view of the animals and the circus people gathered on the wharf. Looking the other way up the ramp, I could see right onto the deck of the spanking new *Royal Tar*.

How thrilling it was when, right past me, circus people and seamen guided the camels, horses, the zebra and gnu, up the ramp to the ship. I watched as they led the animals back along the deck to the stern of the ship where they tethered them under a makeshift canvas roof—crossing the whole width of the ship—for their journey home to America. The *Royal Tar* looked like some strange kind of a Noah's Ark; only this time the sun shone down on all the people and animals and there was no bad weather in sight.

As the large animals passed me up the ramp, I wondered how the ship's crew would find room on the deck for the whole menagerie. But at last, almost all the animals were on board, ready for their journey home. Only Mogul, the giant elephant, wasn't yet on the ship.

Up on the deck, I could see Commander Reed, Saint John's own master of the *Royal Tar*, talking with Mr. H. H. Fuller, master of the DEXTER AND BURGESS circus.

Commander Reed and Mr. Fuller were pacing back and forth along the deck, talking softly together. Commander Reed looked worried. It seemed to me that the crowd on the wharf quietened down for a bit to try to hear what the two important men were discussing.

"Stewart, Atkins, Kehoe!" Commander Reed suddenly shouted to some of the seamen. "There's not enough room for the elephant! Get some men. There's nothing else to do—take these two lifeboats off the ship!

"Oh, and Marshall and McIntyre! Make some stout wooden wedges and put them between the boilers and the deck where that elephant's going to stand. We don't want him crashing through to the engine room!"

A dozen seamen gathered just in front of the main mast. They untied two lifeboats from a platform there. They lifted the bright white boats and began carrying them across the deck to the ramp. Others ran below to make wedges to bolster up the deck to support the colossal weight of the elephant.

At my right, at the foot of the ramp, a noise I heard— or a presence I felt—distracted me. I turned. There, at the edge of the crowd, stood the huge elephant, Mogul.

I leaned forward, putting my elbows up on the ramp, to get a better look. Mogul seemed nervous, shifting his weight back and forth on his massive feet.

Selena stood alone with Mogul, preparing to walk up the ramp to the ship. Surprisingly, she was not in her performing clothes or in working clothes at all. Instead she was in a long dark travelling dress, dressed more like my mother would dress at Christmas and Easter when we went to church in Saint John than a circus lady putting an elephant on board a ship. Strangely, Mogul's old bearded trainer was nowhere to be seen.

So this was it, I thought. Soon I would be waving good-bye to Mogul and Selena and the whole wonderful circus forever. How sad to see them go, yet how exciting—how like a dream—it all had been!

And then the dream turned sour.

Chapter Eleven

Get out of the way, kid!" a voice behind me snarled.

From up on the ramp, someone's boot kicked me in the shoulder, pushing me rudely away from the ramp. I stumbled, bumped into a couple of spectators, lost my balance, and fell down hard onto the dock.

"Mr. Kehoe!" I heard Commander Reed call sharply.

I looked up to the ramp to see who had pushed me. Seamen were carrying the lifeboats down the ramp past a man who stood and watched while the others worked. The sun was behind the man, making him a black silhouette against the sky. When this dark shadow turned to walk down the ramp, I could see that he had flaming red hair and a big stiff flaming red moustache.

But I had no time to wonder who this rough, red-haired Mr. Kehoe was. In a flash, the lifeboats were down on the wharf, the seamen were standing out of the way, Selena was up on the elephant's back, and Mogul was walking up the ramp from the wharf to the ship.

I pulled myself to my feet and squeezed my way back to the edge of the ramp. The ramp shuddered under the great weight of the elephant.

I couldn't believe how gigantic Mogul was up close. His legs, with their huge grey leathery folds, were as big as tree trunks. Tall and wide as a barn wall, he passed right in front of me, blocking out the sun. With a good jump I could have hoisted myself up onto the ramp and touched his short, heavy ivory tusks, or stroked his powerful, sensitive, wrinkled grey trunk.

Mogul was bigger than both our oxen put together, but as I looked up past his long lashes into his small eyes I did not think of the dull slow eyes of the oxen. He was wild and powerful, but his eyes did not put me in mind of the crazed eyes of a hunted bear. No, for some reason, his eyes reminded me of the smart, understanding eyes of my horse.

Yes—I was almost sure of it—this elephant was smarter than anyone guessed. A person could talk to this elephant the same way I talked to my horse. Like all animals, this elephant knew things that people did not know. And a person could learn it all if only he took the time to find out.

Way up on top of the elephant's back, Selena rode sidesaddle in her long dress, looking like some princess riding to a palace in India.

Everybody in the crowd was cheering and clapping as Mogul and Selena marched past me up the ramp towards the ship. I wanted to cheer too, but I had trouble joining in the applause. This was the last I would see of the elephant.

Then, halfway up the ramp, Mogul suddenly stopped walking. On the deck in front of him, the circus band stopped playing. On the wharf behind him, the crowd stopped cheering.

For a moment, it seemed to me as if everything stopped that sunny October day so long, *so* long ago. Time, and the six-thousand-pound elephant, stood still.

I stood up on my tiptoes and leaned over the side of the ramp, watching the elephant stand immobile halfway up the ramp from the land to the ship.

Gently Mogul waved his trunk back and forth. Carefully he gathered the smells of the powerful new steamboat in front of him. Then, finally, deliberately—defiantly, it seemed to me—Mogul jerked his trunk high in the air and trumpeted a long, loud "Nooooooooooo!"

Mogul would not board the *Royal Tar*.

Selena leaned down from her perch on his neck and whispered in the elephant's gigantic grey ear.

But Mogul would not move.

What would happen now?

"Where's his trainer?" shouted Mr. Fuller, the circus master, from the ship's deck.

"Sick!" called Selena. "They've rushed him to the Infirmary. He's got influenza. They'll have to keep him in hospital for a week or two!"

I watched the elephant, three tons of stillness, on the ramp. Why wouldn't Mogul budge? I wondered. What did he know that the rest of us didn't?

"Better get that animal up here!" shouted Commander Reed. "Tide's perfect. Time's a-wastin'! We can be in Portland by tomorrow! Sunday at the latest!"

But Mogul stood stock-still.

Nobody seemed to know quite what to do. Then I heard a shout behind me, at the bottom of the ramp. "Well if nobody else is going to do anything, I will!" the man with the red moustache was snarling. He pushed people aside and barged up the ramp towards the elephant.

At first I backed away from the ramp; I didn't want to get kicked to the ground by Mr. Kehoe again.

"Get goin', you ugly old thing!" the surly Mr. Kehoe snapped as he passed me up the ramp.

"Stand back," Selena said, turning towards the man, but Mogul just ignored the noise behind him and kept staring at the ship. I edged closer to the ramp to see what would happen.

"Well I'll show you then," Kehoe threatened and he pulled a gun from his pocket. Carefully holding the long-barrelled pistol with both his hands, he raised it high above his head.

The crowd gasped. I was shocked. Mr. Kehoe pulled back the hammer with his thumb. I was sure he was going to shoot Mogul. Without thinking, I heaved myself up onto the ramp and started toward the man with the gun.

But it was too late. Before I could get there, Kehoe fired a shot high up in the air, above Mogul and Selena and everybody on the ship.

"Get away, you!" Selena snapped.

"Don't shoot!" I yelled, running towards him.

"Mr. Kehoe!" shouted Commander Reed from the deck of the ship.

"Come back, Son!" my pa called from somewhere behind me on the wharf.

The terrified Mogul wheeled around on the narrow ramp, trumpeting in alarm at the gunshot and commo-

tion. The timbers of the ramp shivered and shook under his great weight.

Mr. Kehoe was scared by the elephant's sudden movement. This time he pointed his pistol straight at the elephant's head.

"Don't do it, Mister!" I shouted.

For a split second, Mr. Kehoe turned towards me. For that one moment, I was afraid he might shoot *me*. But before he or I knew what had happened, the mighty Mogul threw his trunk around Kehoe's waist, lifted him high in the air and hurled him headfirst into the harbour.

Everyone stared into the water.

After a moment, Mr. Kehoe bobbed to the surface, looking like a water rat. The crowd booed. Some of the ship's crew laughed. Commander Reed threw Mr. Kehoe a life ring.

And I suddenly found myself alone and staring straight up into the eyes of Mogul, the "Greatest Beast on the Face of the Earth."

Chapter Twelve

The elephant and I stared into each other's eyes.

I was just a boy, tiny next to the elephant, and shy, just an ordinary boy from a farm in the woods of New Brunswick.

The elephant was an enormous wild animal from far-off India, the star attraction of the DEXTER AND BURGESS circus, famous all the way from New York to Upper Canada, from Nova Scotia to the Boston States.

"Better stand back, Son," Selena said kindly to me.

"He's vicious. He'll kill you," snarled a soggy Mr. Kehoe as he clambered from the wharf up towards the end of the ramp.

But as I looked into the eyes of the elephant, something told me not to be afraid. "Easy there," I said in a soft, calm voice, just as if I were talking to my horse. "Easy, boy." Mogul lifted his large ears away from his head. I could tell that he was listening to me.

I held out my right hand for the elephant to smell. Mogul reached his long trunk out toward me and carefully investigated the scent of me.

And then, while everybody in the crowd waited to see what would happen, I slowly reached into the pocket of my homespun jacket with my left hand. I took out an apple and held it out flat on the palm of my hand.

Mogul moved his leathery trunk towards the other hand, smelled the apple and went to snatch it. But before he could get it, I closed my palm over the apple, stepped lightly past him and started walking up the ramp, the apple still tightly in my hand.

"Come on, Mogul," I said, not looking back. "Giddyap, boy."

To everyone's amazement Mogul followed right behind me. I held the apple hand behind and above my left shoulder. I could feel the elephant's rough trunk tickling my hand, trying to get the apple from me.

"Come on, boy," I encouraged the elephant without looking back at him.

I boarded the ship, and so did Mogul. I walked to the centre of the deck, and Mogul did too. I walked forward towards the front of the ship, away from the stack of hay and barrels of water, up past the two large black funnels to the main mast of the ship, to where I had seen the seamen remove the lifeboats to make room for the elephant. And Mogul followed right behind.

Finally, there, back of the pilot house, between the main mast of the ship and the two great black smokestack funnels, I stopped, turned, and offered the elephant the apple. Gratefully he took it from my hand.

"It's going to be all right," I said to Mogul, reaching up as high as I could to pat the elephant's shoulder.

While I did, two circus men rushed forward and clasped an iron cuff on the end of a very short chain to Mogul's huge left ankle.

Selena jumped lightly from Mogul's back and ran to me. Impulsively she leaned over and kissed me on the cheek. "That was wonderful," she said. "Thank you so much."

And then the crowd went wild, cheering for Mogul, "the Wonder of the East."

Perhaps they were even cheering for me, the New Brunswick farm boy with an apple in his pocket. For circus performers and seamen suddenly picked me up and hoisted me to their shoulders. They carried me back along the deck, accompanied by the cheers of the crowd, and dropped me on the deck where Commander Reed and Mr. Fuller stood watching.

It had all happened so fast. My head was spinning. I did not quite believe that I was really there on the deck of the ship with these people I had watched from afar.

Selena took me by the arm to introduce me to Mr. Fuller and Commander Reed. But just as Commander Reed was about to shake my hand, Mr. Kehoe, sopping wet, was slinking off the end of the ramp onto the deck of the ship.

"Assistant Engineer Kehoe," the captain snapped. "In my cabin. On the double!"

And right behind Mr. Kehoe on the ramp appeared a running figure whom I was overjoyed to see.

"Who are you?" the bewildered captain demanded.

My pa did not even stop to answer the famous master of the new steamer. Instead he ran straight to me. He threw his arms around me and squeezed the breath right out of me in a long bear hug.

"Are you all right?" my father asked, holding me away from him, and examining me to make sure that I wasn't hurt.

"I'm just fine, Pa," I said. There were tears in my father's eyes.

"Congratulations, Son," circus master Fuller said, shaking my hand as if it were the handle of a pump. (Surprisingly, as I saw Mr. Fuller stand next to my father, I noticed he *wasn't* taller than my father at all; in fact, he wasn't nearly as tall as I remembered him in the parade and the circus ring.)

"You've got a fine boy there," Mr. Fuller said, turning to my father.

"That I do," my pa said proudly.

"A strong boy. A smart boy," Mr. Fuller said. "You know," Mr. Fuller said (as if an idea had just dropped into his head out of the blue October sky), "until Mogul's trainer gets better, we sure could use a boy like that in our circus."

The circus master turned to me. "How would you like to work for a circus, my boy?"

Was I dreaming? Could Mr. H. H. Fuller of DEXTER'S LOCOMOTIVE WAX MUSEUM AND BURGESS' MENAGERIE OF SERPENTS AND BIRDS be asking *me* to join his circus?

I turned and looked at Mogul. "I've never worked for a circus before," I said shyly.

"He's needed at home," my pa said firmly. I reckoned that would be the end of the conversation.

But Commander Reed spoke up too. "That's not a bad idea, Fuller. I know I'd rest a lot easier this voyage if I had someone with his way with animals aboard— what with this queer mixture of animals and all. Why I bet the boy would love to make a short voyage—all expenses paid—on the *Royal Tar!*"

I looked at the tall smokestacks and mast of the ship. This *must* be a dream, I thought.

"Pa," I said softly. "I've never sailed on a ship before."

"There's so much to be done at home," my father replied. He turned to the others. "He's all the family I've got."

"I suppose you're right," said Mr. Fuller. "Still, he's such a strong-looking boy, clever and tall." Mr. Fuller slapped me soundly on the back. "And he's certainly good with animals. We'd teach him the ropes, you know."

"Pa?" I asked, hoping he just might change his mind.

"I need you, Son."

"I understand your concern, sir," Captain Reed assured my father. "I have a boy that age myself. I might just mention though that we'll be in Portland tomorrow, and back here by...we'd be away a week at the very most."

"Pa?" I looked into my father's eyes.

After a long silence, he tried to speak.

"I...I'd miss you, Son. You're the only...."

Mogul trumpeted from the front of the ship.

"Mogul likes your son," said Selena to my father. "He'd be just fine."

My father turned and looked at Selena.

"Don't worry," Selena said warmly. "We'd watch out for him. He could borrow some clothes from some of the boys in the troupe. We're like one big family here—he'll fit in perfectly."

My pa put his hand around my shoulder. "Excuse us, please," he said to the others. Together he and I walked away from the others, to where Mogul now stood calmly on the deck.

Mogul reached his trunk out, smelled me and my father, then made a low, contented rumbling with his voice.

"Hello, Mogul," I said.

"I'm proud of you Son," my pa said to me.

"Aw come on, Pa," I said. "Remember the time our ox wouldn't come into the barn? You taught me that trick with the apple."

"Yes," smiled my pa. "But you've got a special way with animals. I never taught you how to talk with them, how to understand them, especially a great savage beast like that. No, your way with dumb creatures— that was a gift from your ma."

We stood there for a moment. Both of us looked up at Mogul.

Gently I broke the silence as I turned to my father. "Please, can I go, Pa?" I asked.

"She was always something with animals," my father said, remembering my mother. "She always wanted to go on a voyage on a ship too. And now, you as well?" Pa asked.

Before I could answer, something wrapped itself around my waist. Before I could do anything to stop him, Mogul whisked me up off the deck with his trunk and held me high in the air.

I gasped for air. All I could smell was the strong foreign odour of elephant. I tried to scream, but no sound came out of me. What was the elephant—fifty times my weight—going to do to me? Squeeze the breath right out of me? Throw me to the deck and dash my brains out?

"Let him down, you big creature," my father yelled at Mogul.

Selena and Captain Reed and Mr. Fuller raced to us, calling to the elephant to let me down.

But Mogul just lifted me higher, teasing them by keeping me out of their reach, playing with me as if I were a toy.

Was he going to kill me?

Selena must have seen the shocked look on my face. "He won't hurt you, Son. He's just playing a game. Stay calm. You'll be fine."

She spoke to Mogul in the same firm voice I had heard her use at the circus. "That's quite enough, Mogul. Let him down."

Mogul hesitated. I dared not breathe.

"Mogul," Selena commanded.

And Mogul, slowly, deliberately, carefully, began to lower me to the deck, gently rocking me back and forth as he did. As I swayed softly back and forth in his grasp, I realized that his trunk wasn't squeezing the breath from me—I had just stopped breathing from fear. His trunk held me tight enough so I wouldn't fall and couldn't get away, but he held me so gently that I could still breathe with no problem at all.

I looked down at the anxious faces below me—my father, the circus people, the seamen, the crowds on the wharf. Mogul's trunk tickled me as he rocked and lowered me and I relaxed a little and realized what a funny sight I must be, and I began to laugh.

I laughed softly at first, then louder and louder, laughing for no reason at all, or laughing for every reason there was—laughing at the wonder of being alive and happy, of being loved by both animals and people.

My father must have thought I was hysterical. "Don't worry, Son. You'll be fine. Don't panic."

But I wasn't scared at all. I trusted the elephant completely. Again and again I laughed!

"Mogul!" Selena ordered firmly one last time. "Let him down."

Mogul mischievously hesitated, then set me down just as carefully as he had picked me up.

I reached out for Pa, still laughing to myself about what the elephant had done with me.

At first Pa just stared at me. Then he couldn't help it either—he laughed with relief and put his arm around me, and then Selena was laughing, and Mr. Fuller and Commander Reed breathed easier and were laughing too when they found out I was unhurt.

"That's some elephant, eh, Pa?" I asked.

"Sure enough is," my father replied.

"You know, Pa, he really scared me at first."

"Hmm. Me too."

"He's so smart. But he was just pulling my leg all the

time," I laughed.

"It looked more like he was pulling your waist," Selena corrected me. And Pa and Selena and I and the circus people and Commander Reed, we all laughed yet again.

"Well, we're going to have to head off right away now," Commander Reed interrupted. "The wind's rising a bit. The time is ripe if we're going to make Portland by tomorrow night."

"Pa?" I asked one last time.

"Yes, Son."

"Please, can I go with Mogul for the week?"

Pa looked at the others. Mogul trumpeted. And then, in a magic moment that pulled the earth out from under my feet, my pa said simply, "Yes, my boy. If your heart is set on it, you can go."

And so I gave my pa a quick hug, and Selena took me by the arm, and before I knew it my father was saying "Be careful, come back quick, Son" and Selena was saying "Don't worry, he'll be just fine" and my father was walking down the ramp, and dreams became real and magic lived...for I suddenly found myself as part of a circus on a brand-new steamship heading out into the great wide world beyond Saint John.

Chapter Thirteen

The powerful *Royal Tar* steamed away from the wharf. Her tall smokestacks belched black smoke; cinders and sparks drifted up into the air from the tops of the funnels, high above the deck of the ship. Beneath the deck, firemen stoked her fireboxes with wood, making the fireboxes glow red hot. Steam hissed out of the valves of her engines as the pressure built up to drive the paddlewheels. Her giant side-paddlewheels splashed, pulling the ship and her strange cargo away from Peter's Wharf and out into the harbour.

What invincible strength this ship had, I thought, as I watched the frothy waves she churned up in the harbour.

The circus band struck up *God Save the King.* The people on the shore whistled and threw their hats in the air and all of us on the deck of the ship waved to all the people left behind.

I walked back to the stern of the ship, past the hay and the water, along the side railing, under the canvas tent that sheltered the animals. I leaned on the taffrail and looked at the crowds on the wharves of Saint John. In that crowd were thousands—probably even the boy with the grey cap and the boy with the fancy suit—who were waving and cheering and watching us go.

But I watched only one person on the wharf, one waving figure on the shore, my pa. As I watched, Pa got smaller and smaller, until finally I could see him no more.

The *Royal Tar* sailed past Reed's Point; downriver past my farm (the unfinished house, nestled in the trees, looked tiny from the ship); around Partridge Island; and onwards into the Bay of Fundy out to worlds I had seen only in my dreams.

Past the shores of New Brunswick and Nova Scotia, the *Tar* headed for the coast of Maine. The circus band played happy tunes, as if this boat ride were one big picnic. Some of the immigrants on the ship danced on the deck to the circus band's tunes.

Then—in no time, it seemed—we sighted Eastport, Maine, and started in to her harbour for a short stop— right on schedule. The band struck up *The Star-Spangled Banner*. The circus people cheered.

For the DEXTER AND BURGESS performers, this was their voyage home after a long tour of Nova Scotia and New Brunswick. But for me, this was my first journey away from my home. This was my trip out into the wide world and the life I would make for myself.

It thrilled me to think of it. It terrified me too.

The warm sun and the cool ocean breeze sent shivers up my spine. I could see New Brunswick no more. I walked forward on the ship to get acquainted with the elephant who had brought me here.

"I'll be home in a few days," I reassured myself. "No more than a week at the most."

It felt good to get down to work that afternoon.

Somehow I felt at home hauling Mogul gallons and gallons of water, pailful by pailful, and bringing him his hundreds of pounds of hay, wheelbarrow-load by wheelbarrow-load, forward from where it was stored. I didn't even mind cleaning up the giant droppings of the constantly eating elephant.

It was fascinating just to watch him chew the hay with his four enormous teeth; to hear the rumbling sounds as the food found its way to his mammoth stomach; to see him suck up gallons of water into his trunk, then curl it around and back to his mouth; to see him spray the water into his mouth and hear the huge gurgling sound as the water went down inside him.

Most of all, Mogul was just plain fun to be with. Whenever I turned my back on him, he would play some new prank on me. Once he threw hay all over my head just after I had brought him some to eat. Once he squirted me with water from his trunk; when I laughed and pretended to get angry with him, he squirted me even more. And often he would lazily tickle my waist with his trunk when I was trying to get some work done.

I also began to learn from Selena how to do tricks with Mogul that afternoon. (She couldn't believe how quickly I learned to work with the elephant, she told me.) Fact is, I was even a part of a circus show that first day away from my home.

Mr. Fuller was giving the passengers of the *Royal Tar* a guided tour around the steamer, showing off all the animals of his menagerie. After the passengers, rich and poor, came up from the animals' quarters below decks, they went to the stern of the ship to see the large animals tethered there. Then they crowded around on the main deck and watched Mr. Jestin do contortions and tumbling and acrobatics.

Then, accompanied by the circus band, all the people came over to where Mogul was chained, and where Selena was teaching me how to work with the elephant.

"Walk up! Walk up! Step right up, Ladeeeees and Gentlemen!" Mr. Fuller called out. "Feast your eyes on Mogul, *elephant extraordinaire*, Mightiest Beast on the Face of the Earth."

"Selena?" Mr. Fuller asked, expecting her to perform on Mogul. But Selena extended her hand in my direction and everyone's eyes were suddenly on me alone.

Just as Selena had shown me, I stepped onto Mogul's big foot. Mogul politely extended his trunk to me. I stood on the elephant's trunk.

"Trunk up, Mogul, lift," Selena commanded. And Mogul lifted me, effortlessly, up, up, up, holding me erect with the end of his trunk, setting me down on the brightly coloured oriental saddle on his back. High above the deck, I held the elephant's sides with my legs, stretched both my arms out straight, smiled my biggest smile, and looked to Selena to see if I had done it all right.

The passengers applauded. Selena and Mr. Fuller applauded too.

Then Selena caught my eye and silently mouthed the orders she wanted me to give Mogul.

Quietly, confidently, I spoke to my elephant friend. "Feet up, Mogul. Feet up!" I ordered. And Mogul lifted first his right front foot, then his left one—the chained one—up onto a heavy wooden box.

"Three cheers for the Amazing Brave New Brunswick Boy," proclaimed the circus master, "the Boy with the Magic of Animals in his Blood."

The passengers cheered again. I beamed with pride.

"Now if any of you kind ladies and gentlemen have enjoyed our modest little show," Mr. Fuller continued, "your kind donations to our humble troupe would be most appreciated." Mr. Fuller began moving among the passengers, holding out his large black hat for donations. But nobody was looking at or listening to Mr. Fuller. Everyone was looking at and cheering for me.

From my perch on top of the elephant's back, I looked down at the people in the audience. Poor children from below the decks and rich children out from their cabins looked up at me in awe.

I don't mind saying I was proud. If my pa and ma could only have seen me then!

Chapter Fourteen

When the sun was going down, and the day's work was done, and most of the people were gone to their suppers, Selena came and sat with me on a mound of hay I had piled next to Mogul.

"What's it like, where you live?" she asked.

"Well," I said shyly, "we live in a small log house on the edge of the woods by the Saint John River. You probably didn't notice it—it looked small from out here—but we passed it this afternoon. The new house, not our old house. You see...."

"Yes...?" she asked.

I had trouble telling even this kind lady the thoughts that stirred inside me.

"What's your life like there?" Selena asked.

"Well, my pa and me, we hunt and we fish, grow hay and potatoes, we look after our oxen and cow and our chickens and our sheep.

"I have a horse all my own," I added proudly. "She's not white like the ones you ride—but she's special, and she's some smart too."

In my mind, I could see my horse as clearly as if she stood beside me. I could see Pa and the home we shared too. It seemed like years, not hours, since I had left my father on Peter's Wharf that morning.

"And the rest of your family?" Selena asked.

"There's just me and Pa," I said. "My mother and

sister—they died."

"I'm sorry," Selena said, as soft as a whisper. "You must love your father very much."

I thought about Pa for a moment. I missed him terribly right then. "Sometimes, in the evenings, about this time or a little later, when our work is done, me and Pa sit by the fireplace, right tired, staring into the fire, just the two of us, all quiet, not saying anything to each other. I think that's my favourite time," I said.

I could hear Selena's breathing. I could feel her bright eyes upon me. I felt embarrassed in front of the famous circus lady. "Your life must be a lot more exciting than that," I said to her.

"Exciting?" Selena asked, with a smile that was not without sadness. "I suppose. I work on the backs of camels and horses and this elephant you like so much. Thousands of people come from all over the continent to watch me and cheer for me. Yes, it's exciting work, I guess, even dangerous.

"But," Selena continued softly, "I spend most of my life travelling from strange town to strange town, from strangers to strangers, always in wagons and boats going somewhere new.

"I have no pa. Nobody else. There's only me. I have no fireplace and even if I did there'd be nobody to sit in front of it with me." For a moment or two, neither of us spoke. "Your mother...?" Selena started to ask me.

But before I could answer, Mogul suddenly made a low, angry, grumbling sound and tugged on his short chain. Selena and I turned to see what was bothering him.

Mr. Kehoe, the red-haired man with the moustache and the harsh face, was sauntering back to the stern of the ship. When he noticed us, he leered at Selena, Mogul and me. Then he wheeled and spat black tobacco juice into the sea and strode past us, along the port rail of the ship.

The man had something evil in his eyes. I heard him laugh from the back of the ship. I shivered. A cold, dark night was coming on.

Later I went below the deck to go to bed in the cramped bunks with the other circus performers. It was dark and crowded and airless down there. My head and stomach felt queer as the ship rolled endlessly in the water. I had a peculiar feeling that something—something I could not name—was wrong.

I went up on top one last time to check on Mogul. I wanted to say good night to my newfound elephant friend.

But Mogul wasn't the calm, playful animal I had come to know that afternoon. He was tugging nervously on his short tether chain. He was listening carefully with his great ears. He was checking the night sea winds with his trunk. He was making a low sound—a complaining growl—that came from deep inside him.

Nothing I tried would calm the elephant.

"Why is he like that?" I asked Selena when she came looking for me later.

"I don't know," Selena said. "Come to bed now. He'll

be all right."

Still I didn't feel right about going when Mogul was so upset. "Please don't laugh at me, Selena, but I think Mogul knows something that we don't."

Selena didn't laugh. "Many times animals know things that humans don't understand," she said. "But what can *you* do?"

"I'm going to sleep here. With Mogul," I said.

"You can't," Selena said. She tried her best to talk me out of sleeping on the deck with Mogul. But I would not be swayed. I had made up my mind. I could not leave Mogul when he was so troubled.

And so, with Selena's reluctant help, I made myself a bed there on the deck, piling a bit of loose hay next to Mogul, under the edge of the platform where the two lifeboats used to sit.

"Are you sure you'll be all right?" Selena asked. "Warmest bed on the ship," I replied with a smile.

Commander Reed was walking by at the time. "Of course it's warm," he laughed. "You're right over the engine room. The heat from the boilers comes straight up through the deck.

"All the same, I don't want some wave washing you off the deck, my boy. There's rough weather coming, I'm afraid. If you're going to sleep there, then tie yourself to the mast."

And so I tied myself to the mast with a heavy rope. I curled up in my bed of hay. I pulled my wool blanket up around my neck. And even though I was in a strange place and far from my home, I slept like a baby for a while that first night away from my pa and New Brunswick.

So much had happened in that one astonishing day. I was wonderfully tired. Every muscle in my body ached. Under my head, under the deck, the ship's engines droned, the ship tossed, and I drifted in and out of my dreams.

Once, I dreamt that my mother came and pulled that wool blanket up around my neck and tucked me in for a long, deep sleep. But when I opened my heavy eyes all I could see was Mogul's huge grey shape above me. I rolled over and tried to sleep again.

But later that night, something reached into my warm hay bed and insistently shook me awake.

"What is it, Mogul?" I asked, looking out from under the platform and up past the elephant's trunk into his small eyes.

I needn't have asked. As soon as I looked out from my shelter, I jumped up from my bed. The ship lurched and I had to hold tight to the heavy rope tied around my waist to keep from being thrown across the deck.

So this was what had been bothering Mogul. A storm was tossing the *Royal Tar* around like a shaving of wood on the waves. The wind blew hard off the shore, from the west, fighting the ship's southerly course, beating the ship with a drenching sleet-like rain.

The port side of the ship rolled up out of the water, and the port paddlewheel pulled in vain against the air. The starboard side plunged deep into the water, and the starboard paddlewheel drowned in the heavy seas.

The *Royal Tar* surged to the crest of one wave, then plummeted into the trough of the next. The whole ship shuddered.

No more the monotonous grinding of engines, no more the hiss of steam, no more the steady swishing of paddlewheels. Now the ship just complained and grabbed, lurched, and frantically splashed in the sea.

My stomach heaved up in my throat. This was not how I had imagined it at all. Like Mogul, I was as terrified as I could be.

Chapter Fifteen

We're taking her in to Little River Harbour!" Commander Reed shouted to me over the roar of the wind, when he came and checked on me later in the night.

The captain pointed, but I could see no harbour opening in the darkness. "We'll anchor her there," the captain said. "How's your elephant doing?"

"Scared," I hollered above the din of the storm. "Me too. Are you afraid, Commander Reed?"

"In a roll like this, we could lose a paddlewheel for sure," the captain explained gravely. "Then we'd have nothing but our mainsail and topsail to get us to shore. They're a great invention, these steamships, Son. But they're not up to much in a sea like this.

"Still, don't you worry, my young friend. The *Royal Tar*'s the newest, finest, strongest steamer on the Atlantic Coast. Put your faith in God, my boy. And in me and my crew. We'll watch her, we'll fire the engine, fill the boilers, check the anchor. And we'll set sail for Portland the minute this blasted gale lets up."

Commander Reed checked the rope that was tied around my waist.

"Your job," he continued, "is to calm that elephant of yours. The last thing we need around here is three tons of panicking pachyderm," he laughed. "Now get some sleep. That's orders!"

But how could I sleep?

Mogul was terrified of the storm, of the way the ship rolled and tossed and crashed down in the heavy seas. He refused to eat or drink. Sometimes his giant body shivered in the cold and damp. When the ship would heave in the sea, he would flap his ears out from his body in alarm.

I tried everything I could to calm Mogul but it was no use. And I was terrified too.

It was a bad dream, our fates depending on this storm—the kind of bad dream I couldn't escape just by waking up.

I closed my eyes and pictured my father in our snug little home on dry land so many miles away. It did no good to wish I was with him there.

But then Commander Reed found the invisible mouth of Little River Harbour, and pulled the ship into its shelter. The ship was anchored, just as Commander Reed said it would be.

Finally I was able to curl up in my bed, snuggling tight under the edge of the wooden platform. Mogul gently pushed some hay in over my blanket.

"Good night, my big friend," I said. "Everything's going to be just fine."

Indeed, I slept a deep sleep through the rest of that night, dry and warm and exhausted, and glad Commander Reed was in charge.

But even Commander Reed couldn't do anything about the weather of the next three days.

Through all of Saturday, Sunday, Monday, the gale

kept raging. For all three days, the *Royal Tar* tugged on her anchor cable. And all that time, the ship's crew and passengers, the circus and the animals, and Mogul and I became more and more anxious to be on our way.

We were running out of food and water for the circus animals; I was only bringing a bit of hay every few hours to Mogul now. The ship was already two days overdue. All of us were short-tempered, impatient to be moving again. Even Mogul, who had been so playful and friendly when we first met, seemed irritable and distant to me now.

Finally, on Monday afternoon, Commander Reed shouted the orders we had all been waiting for. "Fire up the boilers! Pull up the anchor! Full steam for Portland!"

The ship's crew flew into action. Mr. Jestin grabbed one of the band's trumpets and blew a fanfare. All of us on board that ship gave a prayer of thanks and a loud cheer because we were once more on our way! Everything would be all right now.

Outside the harbour our laughing and cheering soon stopped. There was still a heavy sea on. The gale still blew off the land. The engines of the ship still laboured. The paddlewheels still strained.

To everyone's dismay, Commander Reed ordered the ship into Machias Bay. Like everyone else, I did not want to stop and wait. I wanted to get to Portland, and then back home to my pa. But the *Royal Tar*, by captain's orders, was anchored once again.

It wasn't only the weather that was black.

Late that night I was awakened by voices on the deck

at the stern of the ship. The voices were angry and loud.

I tiptoed through the darkness to find out what was going on.

Usually I spent my time on board the ship close to Mogul or down below the decks with the circus performers. Now I had trouble finding my way through the darkness to the back of the *Royal Tar*.

When I got close to the voices I realized that I had better stay out of sight. For there, near the stern, some of the crew sat around talking, and drinking from a small brown crock they passed around.

"The old man's too cautious, that's what!" I heard a familiar voice say. I hid behind a barrel and listened.

"If I were Commander, this tub wouldn't be sittin' in Machias Bay, and that's for certain!" another voice complained.

I was cold and wet. I tried to stop myself from shivering.

"If we hadn't spent all our time tied to an anchor, we'd be in Portland by now!"

"Yeah—and havin' a fine time, I'll wager!"

The men laughed, but there was no joy in their laughter, only hate and drunkenness. I tried to stop my shivering, tried desperately not to make a noise.

"Reed don't know his business, an' that's the truth!" The drunken voice was Mr. Kehoe's...Mr. Kehoe, the ship's Assistant Engineer, the man with the red moustache and the cruel face, the man who had hated me from the moment he first saw me.

"You're just mad because he made you clean the salt

out of the boilers again," taunted another seaman.

"Yeah? Well if he'd have let me keep the pressure up like I wanted, we'd a' been in Portland by now, 'stead o' sittin' in this godforsaken place!" Kehoe snarled.

I tried not to shiver, tried not to make a noise. I started to tiptoe away from the drunken, violent men. But as I backed away from the barrel, I tripped on a large rope and stumbled onto the deck.

The men jumped up. Mr. Kehoe pounced out of the darkness. He grabbed me by the collar and threw me up against the rail.

"Well, well, well," muttered Mr. Kehoe drunkenly. "If it ain't the New Brunswick animal boy." Kehoe's hands tightened around my throat. "You think you're pretty brave, eh?"

"Leave the kid alone," one of Kehoe's mates said.

"Not a chance," snarled Kehoe. "The old man should never have let this queer circus aboard in the first place. It's them what caused this gale—they're Jonahs, every one!"

Kehoe bent me back over the rail, towards the dark seas below. He was drunk. He smelled foul. He grasped my neck so tightly I could hardly breathe.

"Get away from him, Kehoe," another man said.

But Kehoe held on like a leech. "What I wouldn't give to throw you and that ugly elephant o' yourn over-board!" he said maliciously.

Was Kehoe going to kill me? I wondered. Would I never get to Portland? Would I never get home to my pa? Would this black night be my last?

As the storm raged on and the drunken man bent me over that rail, the fury in the black skies and the evil in men's souls seemed stronger to me than all the powers of good—stronger than the power of Commander Reed and the *Royal Tar*; stronger than the circus magic of Mr. Fuller and Selena; stronger than the love between Mogul and me; stronger even than the bond that joined my father and me across all the dark cold miles from Maine to New Brunswick.

But somewhere, far away, as blackness began to smother me, eight bells rang out to signal the changing of the watch. I heard—or did I imagine it?—a woman's voice calling out for me. I heard Mogul trumpet in the darkness.

Midnight. Monday was changing into Tuesday. A new day was being born.

Then, from the pilot-house—could it be real?—the strong voice of Commander Reed echoed through the night. "All hands!" the captain called. "All hands on deck!"

Mr. Kehoe growled to himself, then dropped me to the deck and staggered off. The other seamen instantly became shadows once again.

I picked myself up from the deck and ran, stumbling, terrified, trying desperately not to cry, back to Mogul. I grabbed the front leg of my elephant friend. I buried my head in his massive thigh and reached up and touched his side. All alone, I sobbed, with only Mogul to comfort me.

Chapter Sixteen

We're going to run for it, men!" I heard the captain shout to the sailors assembled by the pilot-house. "The wind's shifted 'round from west to nor'west. She's still a gale, but at least she'll be astern. So fire up the boilers! Haul the anchor! Full steam ahead!"

The crew gave a cheer. I breathed a sigh of relief. Once again we would be on our way.

"Oh, and Kehoe!" I heard Commander Reed shout. "The Engineer's been working all day. You take over now. And check those boilers are full, do you hear?" The wind snatched some of the captain's words from my ears. "We're going straight to Portland...nothing but islands and reefs...not stopping for anything...understand?"

"I'll see that it's done, Cap'n," Kehoe answered, a touch of surliness in his voice.

"Kehoe," yelled Commander Reed, "You fill those boilers yourself!"

And so, the *Royal Tar* raced through the wild night, the strong wind pushing her from astern. Through the black night and into the grey blustery morning, I stood with Mogul on the throbbing deck of the *Royal Tar*.

Unable to sleep, I listened and watched as the terrible power of wind and sea propelled us past a procession of islands and cliffs in that strange grey world so far from my green and brown New Brunswick home.

The calls of the lookout marked our voyage along that desolate coast of Maine...Cross Island...Rogue Bluffs...Head Harbour Island...Winter Harbour...Mount Desert Island...Swan's Island...Isle au Haut....On, on, on we went, on through the murky night, on through the gloomy day.

"Cheer up, lad," Commander Reed said to me late that Tuesday morning. "The worst is over now. That wind'll have us in Portland by midnight—even if we won't be able to hold our dinners down from now 'til then."

Thank Heaven, I thought, as I looked out across Penobscot Bay to Vinalhaven Island. The nightmare was surely ending now. Mogul and I and the circus and the *Royal Tar* were truly on our way. And once we reached Portland, I'd sail straight home to my pa, to our farm, to the place where I now knew I belonged.

Standing up, braced against Mogul, I dozed off into sleep from time to time that endless day on the way to Portland. Mogul's bulk helped me fight against the lurching of the ship. Mogul gave me warmth. Mogul was my friend.

So comfortable was I in my exhaustion that I became mildly annoyed when Mogul tried to push me away, waking me rudely from my sleep. "Stop that, Mogul," I said and tried to fall back into sleep.

But Mogul pushed me again. Something was bothering him. "It's only the storm, Mogul, we'll soon be there."

Still Mogul kept pushing me. I was really perturbed with him now. "If that's the way you feel, I'm going down below for a proper sleep," I snapped. But then Mogul began to destroy my hay bed with his trunk and two front feet.

At first I thought he just wanted to eat the hay of my bed because he was hungry. But he began strewing the hay all over the deck. "Cut that out, Mogul," I said, pushing the elephant away and kicking the hay back into place.

But Mogul wouldn't listen. He trumpeted, and moved the hay once again.

"I'm in no mood for games, Mogul!" I said, leaning over to push the hay back.

And then, for the first time since I had known the elephant, Mogul roughly grabbed me with his trunk and violently shoved me away. For the first time since he had playfully picked me up, I feared the wildness of this animal I thought was my friend. Nervously, I stepped away from the huge wild beast.

Once again, Mogul cleared the hay away, turned to me, and trumpeted loudly. He pounded his foot down on the deck where my bed had been. He tugged at his chain.

Finally, in desperation, Mogul pulled hard towards me, his back leg yanking hard on the end of his chain. He threw his trunk around me, held tight, squeezing me, hurting me, and knocked me roughly down on the deck, right where my bed had been.

For a moment I feared what Mogul might do to me.

But he just stood there above me, looking intensely into my eyes as I lay there on the deck. And then, in a horrible flash, I realized the truth. I jumped from the deck. Where my bed had been, the deck wasn't just warm now. It was burning hot to the touch.

"Commander Reed!" I called as loudly as I could, dashing up to the pilot-house. Breathless, I told the captain everything—about Mogul, about the hay, about the overheated deck.

"Oh God in Heaven," Commander Reed said. He whirled to his mate. "Get Mr. Kehoe up here," he ordered. "On the double!" Commander Reed took a quick look out of the pilot-house towards Mogul.

"What's going on in the engine room?" the captain barked at Kehoe when he sidled into the pilot-house.

Mr. Kehoe looked from the captain to me. "Everything's under control," he replied.

"Did you fill the boilers?" the captain asked.

"Uh, yeah...why?"

"The boy says the deck is hot," said the captain, walking over to Kehoe. "Did you fill the boilers?"

Mr. Kehoe looked at me for a moment, his eyes full of hate. "Who ya gonna believe, Master Reed, a fellow seaman like yerself or some circus kid like him?"

"Did you fill the boilers?" Commander Reed yelled into Kehoe's face.

"I told one of the men to do it," Kehoe said sullenly.

Commander Reed grabbed Mr. Kehoe by the collar. "Are the boilers full, Mr. Kehoe?" he insisted, holding Kehoe against the wall.

"They're a little low, sir," said Mr. Kehoe uncomfortably. "I think you should anchor ship so...."

"We can't anchor here, man! We're most of the way up the channel. Almost on top of Channel Rock. We'd be smashed to a pulp!" Commander Reed screamed. He looked at Mr. Kehoe suspiciously. "How low?" he asked in a whisper.

"Well you'd better do something, Commander Reed," Mr. Kehoe muttered. "There's been a mistake. The boilers are empty."

Commander Reed burst out of the pilot-house. "Stop the engines! Drop anchor!" he shouted over the roar of the wind.

Mr. Kehoe started to slink away.

"Kehoe!" the captain shouted. "Down to the engine room! On the double! Let's get this straightened away, once and for all!"

Commander Reed and Mr. Kehoe headed for the hatch that led to the engine room. I followed right behind them.

"And listen carefully, Kehoe, if you value any of our lives at all!" Commander Reed was saying as they rushed for the engine room. "Open the safety valves on the boilers. Whatever you do, don't put water in them. You pour ice cold water on red-hot boilers, Kehoe, and you'll blow us all to Kingdom Come!"

Commander Reed pushed Kehoe in front of him, down the engine room hatch. "And shut those furnaces down completely," he ordered. "I'm not taking any chances with you this time—I'm here to witness your every move, Mr. Kehoe."

Just as I was starting down the hatch, Mogul bellowed—a loud wild scream I had never heard before, a scream full of the terror of the jungle. The scream echoed through the ship. For a moment there was a deathly silence. Then, above and below the decks, the other animals caught the fear in the elephant's call.

On the deck at the stern of the ship, the horses whinnied in alarm. Below decks, the lions and tigers moaned, birds squawked in panic, the monkeys cried out shrilly—sounding almost like humans in pain.

I ran up from the engine room hatch and across the deck to the elephant.

Where once had been my bed of hay, the deck of the *Royal Tar* was now smouldering and smoking. Darting little flames had already begun to dance from a few of the boards of the deck, grasping on to the stray pieces of hay strewn across the deck, and racing along them to both sides of the ship.

The *Royal Tar* was on fire!

Chapter Seventeen

For a moment, only a moment, I stood transfixed, unable to move or speak, staring at the small section of smoking deck on the *Royal Tar*. Was this how that other fire—that fire in my old log home—started its terrible destruction? Did some stray spark alight on wood and create an inferno that stole my mother and sister from me?

And this fire on the deck of the *Royal Tar* here beside my elephant friend? Had it come to take me to that place where my mother and sister had gone? Was the nightmare repeating itself? Why had fire come back to haunt me again?

I ran to where my bed had been. Frantically I kicked hay away. A tiny flame burst out of a board. I stamped it angrily with my boots.

"No!" I cried, striking the deck with my feet. Another flame jumped up. "No! It cannot be!" I cried, pounding at the flames.

Mogul trumpeted in panic. His ears seemed to stand straight out from his head. "Mogul! Mogul! Follow me!" I called. I started to move away from where the fire was beginning. But Mogul could not run with me; his chain held him tight to where the fire was darting across the deck.

Why was this happening to me? Why to Mogul? And Selena? Mr. Fuller? Commander Reed? The circus people and the seamen and the passengers? All the animals down below?

I did not want to leave Mogul, but as I thought of all the helpless people and animals who could be trapped below the decks, I knew what I must do.

I ran from Mogul, across the deck to warn Commander Reed and all the people on the *Royal Tar*.

"Fire!" I shouted at the top of my lungs. "Fire!" I shouted down the engine room hatch.

Commander Reed rushed up onto the deck. "All hands!" he shouted. "Fire! Fight the fire! Before it's too late!" he yelled.

"Fire!" I shouted down hatches to the circus people and immigrants below the decks.

"McIntyre, hoist a distress signal!" ordered the captain.

"Fire!" I shouted, pounding on the doors of the rich people's cabins.

"You men, stay down there!" Commander Reed called down the engine room hatch. "Join up the fire hoses and man those pumps!"

"Fire!" I shouted as I ran to all parts of the ship. *"Fire!"*

Mr. Kehoe and some other men suddenly came fleeing up from the engine room, bursting onto the deck.

"Get back down there and man those pumps!" ordered   Commander Reed from in front of the pilot-house.

"Impossible!" shouted Mr. Kehoe. "Those wedges you put on the boiler to hold up that despicable elephant—they've caught on fire!"

"Kehoe!" shouted Commander Reed.

"The deck's starting on fire too. It's too hot and smoky down there. There's no way we can operate the pumps and hose—they're useless to us now!" Kehoe snarled back.

"Then get on that bucket brigade!" yelled Commander Reed.

Some of the crew had tied wooden pails and washing basins and small kegs to ropes and were pulling buckets of water up from the sea to throw on the fire. Seamen and circus performers and passengers, rich and poor, had joined together in a line and were passing the buckets of water as close to the fire as they could, then tossing them onto the flames. I got in line too, helping pass the swishing buckets of water to the front of the line.

But faster than buckets of water could be hauled and dumped, flames were leaping and dancing out of the overheated deck above the engine room.

The hungry flames looked for any chance at all to spread over the dry wooden ship. They were gobbling hay, devouring wood, licking their way up ropes and ladders. There weren't enough of us fighting the fire to cut the flames off in every direction.

"All hands on deck!" shouted Commander Reed. Even though seamen had fled the engine room, for some reason the full crew of twenty were not helping to fight the fire.

"Slip the anchor cable! Run the ship ashore! It's our

only hope!" Commander Reed shouted over the confusion and the screams.

"All hands!" he roared. "Cut the anchor cable! Hoist the mainsail and the topsail! Run the ship ashorrrrre!"

I looked to nearby Vinalhaven Island. The anchor cable was cut and the *Royal Tar* was drifting free. Could the sails carry us to the island before the whole ship burned?

"All hands!" Commander Reed shouted angrily again. "Hoist the sails!"

I looked up at the masts and watched the sails slowly begin to unfurl. But there were only a few men tugging on the ropes to get the sails up. Why weren't the others helping hoist the sails to run the ship to shore?

And then, in that split second, while I saw sails unfurl and wondered where the rest of the crew was, I stared in horror as flames jumped up, grabbed hold of the canvas sails, and shot up in a sheet of merciless fire.

"Where are my men?" Commander Reed thundered again.

It was I who saw them first.

The sails weren't up because less than half the crew members were obeying orders. At the stern of the ship, the rest of the seamen—Mr. Kehoe and fifteen of his cronies—had sneaked away to climb into the larger of the only two lifeboats left on the ship. They were lowering the boat over the edge of the ship to get it into the water.

"Commander Reed!" I shouted. "Look!"

"Stop!" commanded the captain, running toward the

lifeboat along the edge of the ship.

I ran to the side of the ship.

"For God's sake, don't take the boat!" Commander Reed shouted to his deserting crew members.

But Mr. Kehoe saw his master coming. Quickly he cut the ropes. The lifeboat plunged into the sea.

"Come back! There are a hundred of us—you can't just save yourselves!" Commander Reed shouted. But the seamen in the lifeboat started to row away from the ship as fast as they could row.

"Row to Vinalhaven!" Commander Reed ordered. "Then come back for the rest of us!" But the men in the lifeboat didn't row against the wind and the sea to nearby Vinalhaven Island. Instead they rowed *with* the wind, in the direction of Isle au Haut, several miles away.

"At least save the women and children!" Commander Reed called desperately after the tiny boat. But the cowardly crew in the lifeboat were looking out only for themselves. They were leaving the rest of us—men and animals and women and children—there on the *Royal Tar*, to die in the blazing fire, to die in the cold, cold sea.

By now, our ship wasn't anchored anymore. Her engines were dead. Her sails were a wall of flames. The wind was pushing us away from Vinalhaven Island.

The *Royal Tar*, the newest, finest, strongest steamer on the Atlantic Coast, would soon be a burning coffin, drifting helplessly out to sea.

Chapter Eighteen

If it weren't for the cowardly flight of Kehoe and his followers, we might have put out that fire on the *Royal Tar*. Up until that point, the fire hadn't spread very far on the deck and through the ship. With the help of the whole crew, we might have got the ship to shore.

But now that the wind was inflaming the sails, now that pieces of burning canvas were spreading the fire around the deck, there was no hope of saving the ship from fire, and little hope of saving the animals and people on board.

Trapped animals screamed in terror. Babies cried. Mothers grabbed their children and dragged them away from the fire. Some passengers still laboured at the bucket brigade but the fire was rapidly getting out of control. It was useless to try to stop the fire now; we must instead find some way to escape from the burning ship.

How could Mr. Kehoe and his friends row for their own safety, while leaving others to perish behind? I wondered. How could anyone be so selfish and evil?

And then I heard a splash. Oh no, I thought with dismay. Someone must have taken the small jolly boat, the only other lifeboat left on the *Royal Tar*, and lowered it into the sea.

I ran to the rail and looked over. There was only one person in the other lifeboat. He was rowing away from the *Royal Tar* as fast as he could. I couldn't believe what I saw! The man abandoning the ship was none other than Commander Reed himself. A couple of passengers at the railing with me called out to Commander Reed, begging him to come back and save them. But the master of the *Royal Tar* rowed steadily away from the ship.

Was Commander Reed no better than the others? I wondered. Could he be deserting us too?

Mr. Fuller and Selena pushed their way through the panic-stricken passengers to my side.

"Thank God, you're safe," Selena shouted over the noise and confusion on the ship. She put her arm around my shoulder.

"How about Mr. Jestin and the others?" I asked Mr. Fuller.

"They all got up on deck," Mr. Fuller replied. "Thanks to you. A good thing too—there's no way we can get back down below now. It's like a furnace down there! We're even cut off from the cabins. Imagine," he shouted, "fifty thousand dollars I've got in a trunk down there—the receipts for our whole season's work. And now I'll never see it again."

I looked out once more towards Commander Reed. He was further than ever from the ship and still rowing. "What's Commander Reed doing?" I shouted to Selena and Mr. Fuller.

"I don't know," Selena shouted back, as confused as me about the master's actions. "But it looks like it's all up to us now."

"Yes!" shouted Mr. Fuller. "Both lifeboats are gone. So are Commander Reed and most of his crew. We're drifting away from the island. The ship won't last long like this."

Suddenly, I heard Mogul trumpet in fear.

"Look!" I shouted. A piece of flaming canvas sail had drifted to what remained of the stack of hay near the stern of the ship. The hay exploded into flames.

"Come on! Let's get the animals overboard!" shouted Mr. Fuller over the pandemonium on the ship's deck. "Perhaps we can save some of them. Maybe they can swim to one of the islands. *They* shall have a chance to live," said the circus master with determination.

"Even if *we* shall not," I thought to myself.

"Go get a sledge hammer and an axe!" Mr. Fuller shouted to me.

I ran as fast as I could to the pilot-house and got the tools. Mr. Fuller, Selena and I fought our way past the burning pile of hay to the stern of the ship. We struggled to knock away a section of railing from the starboard side of the *Royal Tar*. It was almost impossible to wrench the iron railings loose from where they were bolted to the wooden ship, but with the danger of the fire and the threat to the animals, we found the strength to twist and tear a section of the railing away from the side of the ship.

Then we ran to free the large animals on the deck.

Even though the animals were terrified by the fire, we knew that they would not jump from the ship on their own. They would have to be pushed backwards over the edge of the ship.

One by one, the circus people and I led the animals to the break in the railing. We tried to hide our own fear from the animals. We talked to each of them calmly, leading them closer to the break. Then we turned each one at the break so they could not see the dark surging ocean below.

First we pushed the two camels, then the six horses, and finally the zebra and the gnu, backwards into the churning sea. Some of the animals panicked, swimming close to the ship in endless circles around it. But some of them immediately began swimming for their lives towards the nearby islands.

A lion roared in agony from below the deck. Flames shot out of one of the hatches.

"What about the animals below?" I called to Mr. Fuller.

"It's too late for them," Mr. Fuller shouted back. "Besides, they're too wild—we could never let them loose among all these people."

The lion roared again. My throat choked up; I felt the lion's pain.

Then Mogul trumpeted again. "We've got to go get Mogul!" I said to Selena and Mr. Fuller.

The three of us started up towards the centre of the ship. A dozen men were trying to push the circus omnibus over onto its side, to get it to the edge of the ship and to push it into the water to use as a liferaft. Just as they succeeded in tipping it over, the brightly painted wagon caught on fire. A spark, a tiny flame, then suddenly the whole wagon burst into flames. Clouds of smoke poured from its windows, hiding Mogul from us.

I started to run for Mogul, but Mr. Fuller blocked me, grabbed me, held me back. "We can't, Son," the circus master firmly said.

Mogul screamed out. I tugged with all my might against Mr. Fuller.

"The elephant's too wild, too big and strong. He's too frightened," Mr. Fuller said, shaking me to make me listen to him. "Besides," he added, "it's too late."

I tried to see through the inferno of smoke and flames that blocked Mogul from my sight. "No," I pleaded and tried to pull myself free.

By now, Selena was holding me too. Her arms were around me and she, too, held me tight. How I wanted to run to Mogul, but she wouldn't let me go.

"It can't be helped," the circus lady said kindly, and I knew she was trying to fight back her tears too.

Flames were gutting the middle of the ship, forcing everybody to run either to the bow or the stern to get away from the fire and the smoke. The panic and chaos made it seem like there were seven hundred frightened passengers, not seventy, on the ship.

"Come, it's our only chance!" shouted people fleeing madly past us to the stern of the ship.

"Come along," said Mr. Fuller, "there's no time to waste."

"I can't," I sobbed. How long could Mogul last in the raging fire?

And so, Mr. Fuller and Selena took me by the arms and half-carried, half-dragged me from my own dear Mogul, back through the smoke to the stern of the ship.

There, many people crowded along the taffrail. Women held their babies away from the flames and the smoke. Some men tore up planks and hauled ladders, trying to build a raft that could take some of us to safety. Others tied ropes to the ship's rail, all set to climb over the edge of the ship as soon as the flames got too close. Passengers dragged their trunks of belongings out of their cabins and pitched them into the sea in the vain hope they could recover them later.

Suddenly I heard a deafening crash on the deck. I turned and looked to the centre of the ship. Part of the burning masts and rigging and sails had plummeted to the deck. I was sure I heard Mogul scream with pain.

I clenched my fists. I tugged at Selena and Mr. Fuller but I could not get myself free. I closed my eyes and I cried. I honestly wished I were dead.

Chapter Nineteen

T hank God," Selena was saying then. "Look," she was saying and then she was shaking me, "look!"

She was pointing out towards Vinalhaven Island where some of the horses were swimming for shore.

I could see nothing that would make me give thanks.

"Look!" Selena said again.

I followed the line of her finger. There, well out from the ship, Commander Reed had stopped rowing his lifeboat. He stood balanced in the tiny craft, looking through his spyglass, first towards Vinalhaven, then after his deserting crew towards Isle au Haut, then off towards the mainland, many miles away, and finally back towards the *Royal Tar*. Then he sat down in the lifeboat and began to row again—only this time he was rowing back towards the *Royal Tar*.

Was Commander Reed not deserting us after all? Was he coming back to save us? I couldn't believe that he would let all the people on his ship perish in the fire. Was he just making sure no other cowards took the only lifeboat left?

But the jolly boat was too small, I thought, the sea too rough, the distance too far to take us a few at a time to Vinalhaven, rowing against the sea. It would take too long to follow evil Mr. Kehoe and his selfish friends to Isle au Haut for the bigger boat. What could Commander Reed do, what could anyone do, to help all the desperate people and animals on the *Royal Tar*?

"He can't save us all with that little boat," I said despondently to Selena.

"No, he can't," said Selena. "But look beyond Commander Reed—look behind him!"

Then, way off, behind the captain and his tiny boat, I saw what Commander Reed himself and Selena had already seen. From the American mainland, a schooner was sailing towards us. Help was on its way to the *Royal Tar*!

If only people didn't panic, if only everybody could hold on long enough for that schooner to come close, then perhaps Commander Reed could ferry us, a few at a time, to the larger boat and safety.

"Hurrah!" shouted one of the passengers when he saw the schooner approaching.

"Godspeed to that ship!" prayed a mother clutching her baby.

"Let's get these ropes tied and over the edge!" shouted Mr. Fuller. "We can lower ourselves to the boat, or at least hang from the ship until Commander Reed can come get us."

Hope gave us all new strength.

The American ship (the schooner *Veto*, I later found out) sailed closer. Commander Reed rowed steadily towards us. With a vengeance, men went back to lashing their rough raft together. Mr. Fuller and Selena tied ropes for the three of us to the rail, and threw them over the end of the ship.

Frightened passengers screamed in terror, begging

Commander Reed to come save them.

"Don't panic!" Commander Reed shouted over the roar of the fire, the crash of the waves and the desperate cries on the *Royal Tar*. "When I get close, I want five of you to jump overboard! One at a time! Women and children first! But not until I tell you!"

The captain rowed in closer to the stern of the ship.

But then, a sudden gust of wind sent flames racing all up the starboard side of the ship.

A man came running out of the middle of the fire, from up near the rich people's cabins. Frantically, the man was strapping a wide, fat money belt full of silver coins around his waist. The long black tail of his coat was on fire.

Everyone around me screamed. The man jumped up onto the taffrail. The ship tossed and lurched in the waves.

"Don't jump! Not yet!" shouted Commander Reed.

The man teetered on the railing. The ship twisted in the sea.

"Don't!" we all yelled and reached to grab the man back from the rail.

The rich man screamed as the flames burned his skin.

"Roll on the deck!" shouted Commander Reed.

But the man in the money-belt jumped from the rail and plunged down into the cold, rough sea.

We all watched for the man to bob up again. Commander Reed rowed to where the man had gone down. But the silver, tightly tied around the man's waist, was too heavy. A yawning hole opened in the sea and

swallowed the man forever; we never saw him come to the surface again.

"Wait for me!" Commander Reed called. But the fire was spreading too fast.

A gust of wind sent flames racing towards us again. Not far beside me, along the rail, a woman's dress ignited. Desperate, she cried out, hesitated, then—as the flames violently consumed her long dress—she tossed her baby into the sea. Immediately, she dove into the water after her infant.

Someone threw the woman a hardwood plank. She grabbed onto it; it held her afloat. Commander Reed rowed to her as fast as he could. Pathetically, she called out for her baby.

I thought I heard her baby cry. But that was impossible. We had all watched for the baby to surface. The black sea had smothered the baby forever.

Still I thought I heard a baby cry. I listened hard. Smoke and heat and noise and fear confused me.

And then I realized I wasn't hearing a baby at all. It was Mogul, my elephant, screaming oh, so far away.

"Come, Son! Let's go, Selena!" Mr. Fuller called to us. "The wind is pushing the fire this way. Climb over, hold tight to these ropes—we'll hang over the edge and be safe," he said. "For a while at least," he added softly.

But I did not, could not, do as he said. Just as Selena began to climb over the end of the ship, I tore myself free from her grip, turned my back on my circus friends and ran forwards on the burning ship, straight towards Mogul, straight into the heart of the fire.

Chapter Twenty

Smoke surrounded me. Its arms wrapped themselves around me and tried to strangle me. Heat of the fire stabbed at my eyes. Flames jumped and danced and tried to grab me—the same way they had grabbed onto and held my sister and ma so long ago.

Was this how the nightmare would end? Would I disappear in flames like my ma? And my pa—would he be robbed by fire once more?

Somewhere ahead in the maelstrom screamed Mogul. Somehow—though how I did not know—I must save him!

I dodged the flames. I would not let them steal my life from me. I crouched low, away from the smoke. I held my breath, hugged the starboard side of the ship, sliding one hand along the hot rail.

I listened for one sound alone—for Mogul's voice. I followed his desperate trumpeting and hurried along the edge of the ship.

Suddenly, my hand slid off the end of the railing where Mr. Fuller and Selena and I had torn the rail away. Smoke blinded me. Black, empty space opened up beside me, ready to swallow me up, ready to pull me into the cold ocean waves below. Petrified, I fell to my knees.

I crouched there, motionless on the hot deck, blind and helpless, like any of the animals on board that fateful ship, about to die by fire or sea.

And still Mogul's cries called to me.

Inch by inch I ran one hand along the very edge of the ship. Carefully, I crawled behind my seeing hand, towards Mogul's cry.

And then—through good fortune or the providence of God—just as I felt the beginning of the railing at the end of the break, my other hand brushed against the sledge hammer I had left behind a few minutes before. I pulled on the railing to pull myself up. I picked up the hammer and dragged it along the deck behind me.

I would find Mogul! I would use this hammer to set him free!

"Mogul!" I called hoarsely as I groped my way through the thick smoke along the edge of the ship. "Where are you, Mogul?" I cried as I stumbled, lugging the heavy hammer with me.

And then, finally, it was there again—the wild beautiful trumpet call of my elephant friend. It was there, somewhere beside me towards the centre of the ship, towards the centre of the fire, in that inferno of smoke and flame. And Mogul was still alive!

I let go of the rail and held tight to the heavy sledge hammer. I ran, not knowing where I was running, heading only towards the wonderful sound of Mogul's voice. It was practically impossible to see anything through the swirling dense smoke. I had to jump over burning boards and pieces of rigging.

Then—joy, oh joy—I ran right into Mogul, as solid as a wall. I nearly fell over, I ran into him so hard.

"I'm here, Mogul," I called up to him. "Don't worry, boy, I'll never leave you again."

There wasn't a moment to waste. The omnibus behind Mogul had completely burned itself out by now. But pieces of burning rigging had fallen on the frightened animal. And the two tall smokestacks of the *Royal Tar* were now completely on fire, two giant funnels of flame throwing off unbelievable heat and acrid smoke.

Chained as he was, Mogul had had no way to get away from the fire. Where burning boards and ropes had struck him on the back and side, there was a terrible smell of his burnt flesh. Miraculously though, the wind had spread most of the fire away from Mogul, along the deck towards the middle of the ship; nevertheless, I could see that at least one of his feet was badly burned.

Mogul tugged frantically on his chain. Through the smoke I could see his small eyes red and watering. He flapped his ears with fear.

Tears stung my eyes too. I coughed, my lungs full of smoke. I had no idea whether I *could* free Mogul from his chain. I knew only that I *must*.

I lifted the heavy sledge hammer. With all my might, I pounded the hammer against the elephant's chain. The head of the huge hammer glanced off the chain. I lifted the hammer and pounded it down once again.

I pounded and pounded on the chain, but no matter how hard I pounded, the chain would not break.

It was so hard to breathe in the smoke. It took all my strength to lift the heavy sledge, all my strength to pound its heavy head down against the chain and the deck, next to Mogul's huge foot.

In desperation, I lifted the sledge high over my head to let its heavy head fall one last time.

And then, like an earthquake, what was left of one of the huge smokestacks crashed right beside us onto the deck of the *Royal Tar* and over the edge of the ship into the sea.

With a scream of terror, Mogul tugged with all his might to get away from the crashing chimney. The sledge pounded to the deck. The chain snapped. The elephant staggered free, the iron cuff and a short piece of chain still attached to his ankle.

Suddenly released, Mogul almost lost his balance. He turned to me, regained his balance, then seemed to stand still in confusion and fear.

"Oh Mogul," I said, tears streaming down my cheeks. "Come with me now, Mogul. Please come."

I started to move to the edge of the ship. But Mogul did not move; he only looked frantically in all directions at the chaos around him.

He was a pathetic sight, with his burned flesh and singed hair, and his badly burned foot, and his ears out in panic at his sides, and his trunk curled tightly to his body. He whimpered in pain and in fear.

I reached up and gently held his trunk with my hand. "Look at me, Mogul! Look here!" I commanded. Mogul looked down at me, seemed to calm down a little, then curled his trunk around my wrist and arm. We held on tight to each other.

"Now, come, Mogul, come," I said and I tugged on the giant elephant's trunk, pulling as hard as I could, leading him back through the fire and smoke towards the hole in the rail. Over bits of burning debris, around the worst sections of the fire, the two of us worked our way back along the ship.

The shifting wind blew smoke in our faces, then sucked the smoke away. For a split second I was able to see the opening in the rail. With all my might, I tugged on Mogul, guiding him to the opening.

There was no time to lose. Fire surrounded us, ready at any moment to overcome us.

"Turn around, Mogul, turn!" I commanded, turning the great beast around, lining him up with the break in the rail, getting ready to push him backwards over the edge of the ship.

"Back up, Mogul. Jump back!" I shouted. But Mogul stood as still as a rock.

I pushed against Mogul's front legs and chest as hard as I could. Mogul wouldn't budge. "Back up, Mogul, please," I pleaded, tears rolling down my cheeks. Mogul stood stock-still.

"You have to live, Mogul!" I shouted as loud as I could, pounding my fists against his tough hide. "Jump into the water—it's your only chance! Go on! Swim! You mustn't die here, Mogul!"

Once again, I pushed against the elephant. I was gasping for air, coughing on the smoke that burned my lungs. I pushed and pushed. But Mogul would not stir.

"Mogul! For the sake of the good Lord in Heaven,

jump!"

It was too much for me. I pushed one last time, cried out, then collapsed to the deck, falling over one of Mogul's huge feet. My head was spinning. I was overcome with exhaustion and fear, defeated by smoke and pain, unable to fight anymore.

Chapter Twenty-One

In the midst of that hell of smoke and flames, I lay there, perfectly limp, draped over Mogul's colossal foot.

All around me were noise and confusion, death and destruction, all-consuming fire and dense, dense smoke. But to me, what happened around me on the deck of the *Royal Tar* was now like an old dream, a dream I could only vaguely remember.

In my mind, a new dream was being born. I was drifting, drifting, up with the smoke, up from the burning deck of the *Royal Tar*, up past the charred and broken mast, high up from the tiny ship where people and animals ran around in panic, screaming oh so far away.

In my mind's eye, I left that ship far behind and floated through the starlit sky, as light and free as smoke, north along the coast of Maine, past all the islands grey and cold, to a land that was always brown and green, to a place so long ago so far away, a place where ships were pieces of wood a boy pulled beside him in a stream, where fire was something I sat beside with my pa and my ma and....

Sometimes, my dream journey was interrupted by an elephant trunk. (How foolish I had been to try to move an elephant, three tons of stubborn flesh. I was only a boy, a farm boy who belonged at home on the land in New Brunswick with his pa, not alone on the deck of a burning ship in the sea off the lonely coast of a foreign land.)

The trunk pushed at, poked at, prodded me, trying to wake me up. But I wanted only to sleep, drift far from the struggle and pain, take a long and quiet journey back, or ahead, a journey to a simpler land....

Sometimes hands, cool hands, tried to shake me from my dream. Hands, soft hands, a woman's slender hands, holding my shoulders, stroking my face, lifting my back from the burning deck. But I wanted only to go, let go, go....

I may have heard a voice, a woman's voice—an angel maybe, my mother so long ago, a beautiful circus lady I once knew, Selena, Selena...whoever she was, calling me home, lifting me up...a voice saying, "Mogul! Lift!"...trunk prodding, trunk enfolding, trunk squeezing, trunk lifting...lifting me up and setting me down, on the pretty saddle on the back of the elephant, in the picture on the poster on the tree...down on the strong elephant's back, my body slumping forward on the strong elephant's neck, my arms draped down at the strong elephant's sides...the voice saying, "Mogul! Turn!"...the elephant turning now, the kind voice comforting, me rocking on the strong elephant's back like a baby...the voice softly calling me come, come, come..."Mogul! Feet up! Feet up! Up on the rail!"...the elephant's huge front feet going up now, up on the rail of the ship, first one foot...me sliding down on the elephant's back, my hands instinctively grasping the thick folds of skin on the elephant's neck, the warm, tough folds of skin...one foot up on the rail of the ship...the voice yet again..."Mogul! Feet up!"...one foot, then two, the strong elephant going up, up, all his great weight on the rail...me, the New Brunswick boy, on the elephant's back...the elephant's prodigious weight on the rail of the ship...up, up, up, then—

CRASH!—the ship's railing giving way under the elephant, the elephant and me plummeting down, down, down through space, rush of air, cool blast of wind, then—

SPLASH!—Mogul and I plunging deep into the cold black tomb of the sea.

The shock of the cold water snapped me violently out of my dream. The water closed over my head and tore me from Mogul's back. I gasped for air but swallowed only sea water instead. Desperately, I flailed my arms and legs, and shot up to the surface of the water.

I tried to call out but all I could do was cough bitter salt water out of my lungs.

I thrashed around with my arms and legs, trying to keep my head above the tossing surface of the water. But the ocean threw me about like a helpless piece of flotsam.

I could see no sign of my elephant friend.

A huge wave crashed over my head, pushing me under the water once more. Again I flailed, pulled myself to the surface, gasped for air, and tried to keep my head above water.

Suddenly I saw Mogul. His great round back broke the surface of the water far from where he had gone down, and he emerged, looking like some monster of the sea or an overturned boat.

Mogul lifted his giant head and trunk high out of the water. He sprayed water violently out of his trunk.

"Mogul!" I called. I reached my arms out towards the elephant. Mogul turned to me and trumpeted long, loud and strong.

A third wave crashed up over my head. The powerful ocean was pulling me down for the third time. Just as the fire had swallowed my mother, the sea was swallowing me for good now, smothering me, sucking away my breath forever.

But before my life slipped completely away, Mogul reached out his trunk, squeezed it tightly around me and pulled me back to the surface of the ocean. Up into the world of air Mogul pulled me, rescuing me from the deadly grasp of the sea.

I threw my arm over his neck and grabbed onto folds of his skin. With my last strength, I hoisted myself up onto Mogul, threw my legs over his neck, and clung to his hide for dear life.

"Oh, Mogul," I sobbed with relief. Miraculously, both Mogul and I were safely off of the burning ship. Now if only we could make our way to land.

I took one last look up at the burning *Royal Tar*. There, where Mogul and I had been only moments before, the ship was a furnace of smoke and flames.

And there—to my surprise—by the twisted, broken railing of the dying ship, in the middle of that fiery nightmare, stood a woman...Selena, no dream, but the kind circus lady who had saved me from death on the deck of the *Royal Tar*.

Chapter Twenty-Two

J ump, Selena! Jump!" I screamed at the top of my lungs.

Selena stood at the very edge of the ship. All around her was fire and smoke. She had come forward on the ship to save me and Mogul, and now because of it, fire cut her off from the stern of the ship, where Mr. Fuller and others hung from ropes. Fire cut her off from the bow as well.

Commander Reed's lifeboat was far from the ship now, carrying another few passengers to safety on the American schooner *Veto*. There was no safety in the swirling waters below Selena. But if she stayed where she was, she would surely perish in the fire.

"Jump, Selena!" I called again.

Still Selena hesitated, standing poised on the edge of the ship. Mogul swam back and forth, staying close below her. I held tightly to his back.

Then, suddenly, without warning, Selena's clothes and beautiful long blonde hair caught fire.

"Please, Selena, *jump!*" I called to the woman who had risked her life for mine.

At last, Selena dived, straight into the water near Mogul and me. As she surfaced beside us, I could see that her beautiful hair was singed but she was alive. I was oh, so glad to see her.

Mogul turned and swam towards Selena. I reached

out my free hand towards her, holding tight to Mogul with my other hand. Her heavy, soaked dress was pulling her down but she swam strongly through the waves towards us. I caught her hand. With all my might, I pulled her up behind me, up onto the elephant's back.

The waves were crashing all around us. I leaned forward and held tightly to Mogul's neck. Selena squeezed close behind me and put her arms around my chest. And Mogul turned and swam, carrying the two of us through the cold, rough sea, away from the burning ship.

Looking back, from the water, the *Royal Tar* was an awesome sight. The fire raged on board, consuming anything that would burn. The wind and the sea were pushing the powerless wreck further and further away from Vinalhaven Island, out towards the cold, unprotected Atlantic Ocean.

Not everyone would be as fortunate as Selena and Mogul and me. At both ends of the ship, people dangled from ropes. Above them, fire leapt out to burn their ropes. Below them, the ravenous sea grabbed at them, trying to tear them from their ropes.

As we rounded the stern of the ship, I watched helplessly from Mogul's back as an old woman's rope burned through. The tiny old lady dropped into the sea. She bobbed to the surface. A man hanging from a rope reached down with his legs to try to grab the woman. But a wave tore the old woman away.

Fortunately, the next wave washed the woman up

against the ship. A second man hanging from a rope grabbed the old lady with his legs, holding her slightly out of the water. But how long could the tiny old woman hang on, waiting for help?

I could recognize Mr. Fuller by his long black coat. He hung from a rope tied to the tiller chain at the stern of the ship. A man and two children shared Mr. Fuller's rope with him.

In the water, people who had jumped from the ship or fallen from their ropes valiantly held on to bits of plank from the ship, pieces of the deck or spars, the makeshift raft, waiting desperately for Commander Reed to save them from the greedy sea.

Meanwhile, Commander Reed and two of his loyal crew members were rowing the tiny lifeboat non-stop through the heavy seas, back and forth from the *Royal Tar* to the American schooner. I saw Commander Reed reach out his oar to pull in a swimming woman who cried out in desperation. The woman had lashed her baby to her body with a rope. Commander Reed pulled the woman and her baby aboard his already heavily laden boat.

Why didn't the *Veto* come closer to the *Royal Tar*? I wondered. Why didn't the *Veto* send out lifeboats to help? (The *Veto* only had two tiny boats, neither big enough to help, I found out much later. The *Veto* also had gunpowder on board so its captain feared getting too close to the fire. But why didn't they throw the powder overboard and come closer to the burning ship? I still wonder to this day.)

How long could the survivors of the *Royal Tar* hang on? How long could Commander Reed keep going? And how long before the ruined *Tar* sank to the bottom of the sea?

From up on the burning deck I heard one lone voice eerily singing a hymn. I shut my eyes tight and begged God in Heaven to come down here to help Commander Reed and all the poor survivors of the fire aboard the *Royal Tar*.

Meanwhile, Mogul, as big and as strong as a boat, pushed his way steadily through the waves, his two waterlogged passengers holding tightly to his back. Despite the fire and his burns, despite his fear, Mogul, strong and solid, his trunk thrust high out of the water, left the *Royal Tar* far behind, and swam, not against wind and waves to Vinalhaven Island, but with the wind and the waves towards Isle au Haut, still a long, long way away.

Selena and I shivered with cold. The long afternoon of the fire was over, and night—my fifth night away from my pa and my home—was coming on. Once, only once, I looked back. The *Royal Tar* burned red against a purple sky. Like the sun, the *Royal Tar* would soon sink into the ocean. The sun would come up again; the *Royal Tar* would not.

For an hour, maybe two, Mogul swam. He was a mighty swimmer. But he was also exhausted, cold and afraid. In addition to his own weight, he carried us two humans on his back. The rough waves fought against him endlessly. Isle au Haut seemed to be miles from the wreck of the *Royal Tar*.

Selena and I held tightly to each other, and pressed ourselves against our elephant friend. Waves splashed up over our bodies and faces, making us wet and cold. Under the water our legs became drenched and numb. The cold night winds robbed what little body heat we had left.

Mogul, so silent and strong, was tiring now. Beneath us he shuddered with the cold. He was slowing down. He had to strain more and more to pull the three of us through the heavy seas.

Clouds raced past the moon, erasing light from the world. Darkness, wet and cold, pressed down on us three lonely survivors from the *Royal Tar*. There was no way of knowing how far we were from land.

Was this how it would end for the three of us? I wondered sadly. Had we survived the gale, the villainy of Mr. Kehoe and his gang, the conflagration of the

Royal Tar, our hours together in the ocean, only to drown, lost at sea, when Mogul could carry us no more? (For, friend, there is no earthly way that Selena and I could have swum those terrible miles to shore if Mogul had given up on us then.)

Was this how my dream about a wonderful circus elephant and a beautiful circus lady would come to an end? Would we—friends all three—sleep our sleep of death on the bottom of the sea?

"It's all right, Mogul," I whispered in my elephant's ear. "You tried your best." I thought of all the elephant had done for me. "I love you, Mogul," I said softly.

Though my body was too numb to feel much pain, my heart hurt like an open wound. This was, I sensed, the beginning of the end.

But something, a shadow in shadows, moved with us through the water and the night. I peered through the darkness beside us. Could this shadow be real?

"Look, Selena. Look, Mogul," I whispered, pointing.

There beside us sailed a ghostly ship, heading with us towards Isle au Haut, somewhere up ahead. Could it be the American schooner? I wondered. Might Commander Reed be on board? With what survivors? Mr. Fuller and Mr. Jestin? The people who were hanging on the ropes? The people who were floundering in the sea?

"Help! Help us!" Selena and I called weakly. But the ship slipped past us in the night.

Still, the ship's presence gave Selena and me new hope. It seemed to give Mogul new strength. He swam, pulling hard, following the shadowy sailing ship, carrying Selena and me towards the safety of the shore.

The ship disappeared ahead of us. But Mogul kept swimming. He kept smelling for land. And finally, his huge feet struck bottom there off the shore of Isle au Haut. One at a time, he lifted his heavy feet through the water, plodding with determination into the shallows, lifting Selena and me higher and higher out of the water, up onto the rocky beach.

I looked around me in a daze. My brave elephant had made a miracle happen—he had brought us safely to land!

Chapter Twenty-Three

Now high on the rocks of the shore, Mogul, the once-mighty elephant, limped a few steps, then collapsed to his knees, the huge bulk of his exhausted body sinking to the ground. Selena and I jumped clear of his back, afraid he might roll over on us.

Once out of his way, Selena and I also crumpled to the ground.

Instantly, I closed my eyes and curled up like a baby, trying to protect what little warmth I had from the cold wind that threatened to steal it from me.

The wind rushed through the trees behind us. The sea crashed against the lonely shore. But for me, the beating of my heart was the loudest sound that I could hear.

How long we lay there I cannot tell you. All I know is that the rocks and ground, solid and hard, so unlike the everchanging sea, felt good to us then. But we all knew, I think, that we must stir ourselves to get up and seek help, or risk dying there on the cold rocks.

Mogul coughed feebly, trying to clear his lungs of sea water. Wearily, I turned my head and opened my eyes enough to look at the elephant who had saved our lives.

Poor Mogul lay fully over on his side now. He was completely worn out. He was soaking wet and trembling with cold. He was having difficulty breathing.

"Selena," I said. She rolled over weakly and looked

at me. "Is he going to be all right, Selena?" I asked. "He looks so sick."

Selena looked at Mogul. "Oh no," she said as soon as she saw him. "Come, help me!" she said with urgency, and found the strength to pull herself to her feet.

"What is it?" I asked. The last thing in the world I felt like doing was getting up. I had no strength left.

"Get up," Selena told me sharply.

I reached out to a rock. With great effort, I pulled myself up to kneeling.

"He mustn't lie down!" Selena said. "He's too heavy. If he lies down for long his weight could crush his lungs and he'd die!"

Mogul coughed and breathed heavily again.

With rubbery arms and lifeless legs, I forced myself to stand. I stumbled over to Mogul with Selena.

"Come on, Mogul, get up!" I commanded.

"Mogul! Stand!" Selena ordered.

The elephant grumbled in a voice that came from deep in his chest, but he made no effort to move.

I leaned over and put one hand gently on the elephant's huge neck. I put my face down to his giant ear and whispered to my friend, "You did it, Mogul, we made it. Come along, now, boy, we're safe. Get up now, Mogul!"

Mogul sighed as if he were falling into a deep sleep. He did not stir himself.

"He *must* stand or he will die," said Selena.

"Help me, Selena," I begged. The two of us got behind his shoulder, put our hands under it, and tried to lift with all our strength.

"Get up, Mogul! Stand! Come on, Mogul! Get up!" we insisted as we shoved against the unmoving mass of our elephant friend. But there was no way we two mere humans could move a creature fifty times our weight.

"I won't let you die!" I said, almost angrily. "You saved our lives, Mogul. Now get up! Please!"

I looked to Selena. I could see in her eyes that she, like me, feared that Mogul was giving up. He would struggle no more to stay alive.

How could I change Mogul's mind? How could I tell him to stay alive? How could I make him get up?

I remembered how this strange huge creature had told me about the fire on the ship. Though I did not understand what he was trying to tell me then, he did not give up until I had felt, like him, the heat building up on the deck. I remembered his trunk around me, throwing me violently down to the deck of the ship, ready to do *anything* to make me understand. He did not give up on me then; I could not give up on him now.

I knew we could not push him up. We must make him want to stand, we must force him to get up and live.

I ran around in front of his face. Firmly—almost angrily—I shouted at him, "Mogul! Get up!"

He did not even open his eyes.

"Get up! Stand up!" I shouted, and with my foot I gave him a firm shove on the shoulder, being careful not to touch the huge burned welts on his side.

Half-heartedly, as if annoyed by a mosquito, he jerked his trunk to brush me away.

"Stand!" I shouted, and shoved him roughly with my foot once again.

"What are you doing?" Selena asked me in surprise.

Mogul batted at me with his trunk.

"Come on, Mogul!" I shouted. "I will not let you lie there and die!" I pushed him hard with my foot once, then pushed him hard again.

The elephant's eyes opened. He growled a deep growl and tried to keep me away with his trunk.

I would not give up on him. I would wrestle him if I had to.

"Get up, Mogul! Right now!" I screamed and moved down his side where his trunk couldn't reach me, shoving his leg with my foot, prodding his side with my foot.

Mogul tried to get at me with his trunk but I was too smart for that. He tried to kick me away with his heavy feet but I was too quick for him. He rocked up a bit on his side to try to slide around to reach me. He was getting angry now.

"Stand, Mogul! Stand!" I shouted and now I was behind him, prodding him, pushing him, poking him in the rump and starting along his back. "Get up, I tell you, get up!"

Mogul trumpeted a screech of annoyance and threw his trunk back, trying to strike me. I jumped out of his way.

"That's it, Mogul! Come now, get up, come and get me!" I yelled and I started shoving violently at his back. Now Selena, holding her heavy wet dress in her hands, joined in, pushing at the elephant's back and sides with her feet, and Mogul had two of us to bat away.

"Stand up!" ordered Selena and "Get up right now!" I insisted, and we both shoved at the elephant with our feet, and Mogul, angry now, rocked up on his side a little, then rolled back down.

And we shoved and we prodded, and he rocked up again on his side, a little bit higher this time, and rolled back down on his side once more. And we shoved and he rocked, back and forth, back and forth, rocking himself up onto his side and screeching his annoyance at us, and we shouted and he rocked and rocked—like he was having a mud bath in India and not lying on cold, wet rocks in Maine—until with one giant heave of his body that seemed to shake the very ground we stood on, he rocked his whole huge self up onto his tree-trunk legs, and whirled his whole huge bulk around to attack the pesky humans who were annoying him so much.

But Selena and I wanted no fight with our elephant friend. We were so glad to see Mogul on his feet that we let out a great cheer that stopped Mogul in his tracks.

"Hurrah for Mogul!" we called. "Good for you, Mogul!" Without fear, we ran to him. We buried our heads in his huge front legs and held ourselves close to him.

Now we were facing the land, looking towards the dark shadowy woods behind Mogul. But Mogul, newly back up on his feet, was facing out to sea. While we were celebrating our elephant's return to the land of the living, Mogul raised his trunk and blew a long sad call.

Selena and I turned and looked out with Mogul to the

sea.

Out on the horizon, tiny in the vast expanse of the sea, but bright in the darkness of the night, what little was left of the *Royal Tar* was dying. Flames and smoke poured up one last time from the ship, lighting up a tiny patch of dark purple sky. The bow of the steamer rose flaming towards the heavens. The stern sank silently into the dark waters. The *Royal Tar* cut into the sea like a red-hot knife and disappeared from sight, gone to her grave in the ocean deeps. The strongest steamship on the Atlantic Coast was now nothing but a puff of steam.

A cold moon looked on from the violet sky.

Chapter Twenty-Four

For a moment we watched in silence. No words could tell what we felt as we watched the ship, knowing that some—perhaps most—of her animal and human passengers were going down with her.

"*We're* alive," said Selena, breaking the silence.

"Thank Heaven for that," I said, reaching up and stroking Mogul's side. I turned and looked towards the land. "But where do we go now?"

Uncertainly we walked up to the edge of the woods and looked both ways along the shore. We could see no lights or roads along the curving rocky beach of this island. Left or right through the darkness? Which way would lead us to help?

Mogul decided for us. With a quick check of the smells in either direction, he turned to the left and began walking his slow, determined, lumbering walk, favouring his burned foot, along the shore. He continued walking, every so often raising his trunk, checking smells. Selena and I followed him.

Then something—a sound perhaps, a smell, a feeling, a memory of someone he loved or hated—something made this elephant who had lain lifeless on the ground a few minutes before start to speed up. His heavy feet hit the ground quicker and quicker, and he began running in a rolling one-foot-at-a-time charge through the darkness.

"Mogul!" I called weakly. "Slow down. Where are you going?"

"Wait for us!" cried Selena.

But we both knew that once Mogul's mind was made up, it was almost impossible to change it. So instead of trying to get him back, we ran, as best we could, to catch up to the elephant.

We were hungry and exhausted, but more than anything else we were cold right through. After a while, it actually felt good to run. Even though we were still soaked and the night wind blew cold, running along the shore helped warm us up.

And then we came to a point of land and found Mogul standing, waiting impatiently for us. The uneven rocks and pebbles of the shore suddenly changed to a packed mud road that led along the edge of the woods. A road, we thought, must lead somewhere. And, unlike the exposed ocean beach, the woods sheltered us from the wind.

Mogul's road did lead somewhere. Running and stumbling, as tired as we could be, the three of us rounded a bend of the shore and suddenly, there in front of us was a fisherman's hut, warm and welcome, candlelight spilling from its tiny windows.

We stopped, stood still, and stared in disbelief at the welcome cottage and the small barn attached to its side.

"Selena, we did it!" I shouted. We threw our arms around each other in joy. "We made it, Mogul!" Ecstatically I jumped up and patted his side. "Now come Mogul, Selena, come quick!"

I ran to the door of the fisherman's hut, Selena and Mogul close behind me. I jumped up on the open porch and pounded on the door of the hut, a poor simple house like my home in New Brunswick. I pounded again. "Help us! Please open up!" I called.

The door opened slowly, just a crack at first. "Please help us," I blurted out. "We're survivors of the *Royal Tar* that burned and sank offshore between here and Vinalhaven Island this very night!"

A bearded old fisherman opened the door the rest of the way and held a candle up to my face. He stared at me and my two companions behind me—a drenched and exhausted boy, a shivering circus lady with charred hair and a saturated dress, and a mammoth scarred elephant, all standing outside his hut on that isolated island in Maine. He stared at us as if we were ghosts.

"The *Royal Tar*?" the old fisherman asked. "Are you really alive? Or are you some spirits, back from the dead?"

"We're alive," I answered, puzzled at the old man's look of fear. "But please—we need help."

"But *they* said...." The old man turned back to look into his house.

Selena, Mogul and I looked too. There, sitting at the fisherman's table and standing around the edge of the room, eating and drinking, comfortable, safe and warm, were Mr. Kehoe and his traitorous followers.

"Mr. Kehoe!" I blurted out.

The men at the table, as surprised as we were, jumped up from their places at table.

Too angry to be afraid, I walked past the old fisherman right into his tiny house. "Murderer!" I said to Mr. Kehoe.

"You lily-livered cowards!" said Selena, and the two of us approached the trapped, guilty seamen who had abandoned us all on the *Royal Tar*.

"What's going on here?" asked the old fisherman.

"I didn't do anything," Mr. Kehoe snarled, and belligerently he took a step towards us.

"We know you didn't do anything," I said, not backing down from that bully. "You didn't do anything to help the women and children who drowned and burned back there on the ship. You didn't do anything to help the trapped animals below the deck. You didn't do anything to help Commander Reed or the *Royal Tar*."

Kehoe moved towards me as if to strike me with his clenched fist.

The old fisherman intervened. "I don't understand. What happened out there?" he asked Kehoe and his men. They said nothing so he turned to Selena and me. "These men said...."

From behind, Kehoe rudely pushed the frail old man out of his way. The old man fell to the floor. Kehoe lifted his clenched fist against me again.

And then, behind me, there was a splintering crash outside the fisherman's front door. All of us turned.

Mogul had stepped up onto the fisherman's porch and had crashed right through it. His giant head leaned down and poked through the tiny door of the fisherman's hut, filling the whole doorway. Mogul growled his hatred at Mr. Kehoe. He looked as if he would squeeze into the room or pick up the whole house if Kehoe so much as laid a finger on me. Believe me, it was worth seeing the look on Kehoe's face then.

"What's this all about?" the fisherman asked, trying to pick himself up from the floor.

Kehoe and his men, trapped and guilty and faced with the wrath of the elephant, retreated towards the back door of the fisherman's hut. Mogul growled again and Selena and I approached the men.

Then, from inside the pocket of his coat, Kehoe took out his pistol and pointed it in our direction. I took a step towards him. Kehoe pulled back the hammer of the pistol with his thumb. Selena held me by the arm to stop me from pursuing him.

"It's Commander Reed's fault this all happened, not mine," Kehoe said. His two hands held the long-barreled pistol steadily pointed at us, while he let his men escape one by one out the back door. "His fault and the fault o' that circus o' yourn."

Kehoe started to follow his cronies out the back door. No sooner had I started to step towards the door than he pointed the pistol back through the door and straight at my head. "And I'll kill anybody what says otherwise," he said. He fixed me with his cold eyes, then slithered out the door.

Chapter Twenty-Five

As soon as Kehoe was gone, Selena and I helped the poor fisherman to a chair, then ran and cautiously looked out the back door of the house.

By the light of the rising moon, we could see Mr. Kehoe and his men starting to cross the field at the back of the fisherman's hut. As they walked they were looking nervously back over their shoulders. All of a sudden they began to speed up. Mogul had gone around the house and was pursuing the men.

"Call off that beast!" Mr. Kehoe shouted to Selena and me. He turned and pointed his pistol at the approaching elephant. "Call him off or I'll shoot."

"Stop, Mogul," Selena called as she walked from the house into the field.

"Mogul. Stop!" I called.

But Mogul had made up his mind.

In the moonlight, Kehoe took aim and fired his gun at Mogul. But Kehoe's shot went wide.

For a moment, Mogul stopped; I breathed a sigh of relief and prayed that Mogul would stay safe with us and that Mr. Kehoe would take his gun and his evil ways and leave us forever.

But Mogul was determined to make sure that Kehoe would leave us alone for good. He walked again, slowly at first, then faster and faster towards Kehoe and his gang. Most of the men turned and began running as fast as they could over the rough mud and stubble of the field. But Kehoe dared not turn his back on Mogul; he stumbled half-backwards across the field, his gun pointed at the elephant.

"Call 'im off, I say!" Kehoe cried.

"Stop, Mogul!" Selena and I both called. Mogul kept walking. Kehoe aimed his gun. We ran to stop the elephant.

Mogul lumbered steadily towards the man, growling his hatred, his huge feet making the ground tremble.

Kehoe shot at the elephant again, but this time tripped on a clod of earth and fell hard into the mud. Mogul was almost upon him.

"Stop, Mogul!" I yelled. "Kehoe, don't shoot!" I ran to catch up to the elephant.

Most of Kehoe's men were now safely across the field and were starting down a road through the woods on the other side. But the fallen Kehoe had only his gun between him and the fury of Mogul.

"Get away!" snarled Kehoe as Mogul charged towards him. From point blank range, Kehoe shot at the elephant again, then clambered to his feet and began to run.

For a moment the mighty Mogul hesitated in his run, broke his stride, and screamed out in pain. I knew he had been hit.

"No!" I cried and—with no thought for my own safety—dashed up beside Mogul.

But Mogul began to run after the fleeing Kehoe.

"Wait," Selena called behind me.

I had to stop Mogul before he got shot again. I ran as fast as I could, trying to get ahead of him. Blood was flowing from a bullet hole in his shoulder.

"No, Mogul, let him go," I shouted and I jumped and grabbed on to the folds of skin on his front shoulder, trying to stop and save him.

"Stop, Mogul! Stay here! He's not worth it!" I cried. But Mogul kept going, dragging me—my feet off the ground—right along with him. Kehoe was scrambling across the field. Mogul, practically breathing down his neck, trumpeted shrilly at the evil man.

The terrified Kehoe whirled around and fired his pistol once again.

"Watch out!" Selena shrieked, from behind my elephant and me.

Suddenly I felt a sharp, piercing pain in the back of my shoulder.

I cried out in agony. I dropped to the ground, landing on my feet in front of Mogul. Mogul stopped dead in his tracks, careful not to trample me.

I clutched at the back of my shoulder. I felt something hot and sticky and a sharp, sharp pain. My knees went rubbery, my head began to reel. I felt like I was going to fall to the ground.

Selena caught me and supported me under the arms. Mogul's long trunk reached down and smelled my blood.

Then Mogul seemed to go completely wild. He trumpeted angrily, fiercely, shrilly. He looked up and saw Kehoe scrambling across the field to escape by the road.

Mogul stampeded after Kehoe.

Mr. Kehoe stopped running, turned and shot once more. He narrowly missed the elephant but Mogul charged without hesitation. Kehoe fired again. Mogul kept stampeding towards the red-haired man.

I heard Kehoe pull back the hammer of the gun with his thumb again. I braced myself for the gunshot. I heard Kehoe squeeze the trigger. But this time no gunpowder exploded and no bullet flew through the air.

A wave of terror crossed Mr. Kehoe's face as the elephant approached him. In desperation, he threw his useless gun at Mogul. "Help!" he shrieked. He turned and fled towards the road. Mogul chased after him, shaking the earth and trumpeting his anger at the man.

Kehoe and his men were running down the dark road into the night. Mogul was charging after them. "Save me from this beast!" I could hear the running Mr. Kehoe call.

I tried to pull myself away from Selena. "Mogul," I tried to say, "I have to get Mogul."

But already the night stars were spinning. The face of Selena was blurring. Everything was getting so hot and dark and confused.

Mogul was chasing Kehoe into the night. And I was getting lost in blackness.

In my confusion, I seemed to walk without doing the walking myself, one arm over the shoulder of Selena, back to the fisherman's hut.

Then, without knowing how it came to be, my other arm was over someone else's shoulder and my feet dragged along with theirs.

There were voices then, familiar voices...Mr. Fuller? Mr. Jestin? Commander Reed? I must be dreaming, I thought; it was impossible those voices could be there. I struggled to open my eyes; strange faces spun around me in the darkness.

"Selena," one of the faraway voices was saying, "You're safe...we heard the shots...what happened?...Mogul?...The boy?..."

"Mogul," I tried to say. The voices were fuzzy. I could not focus on the faces around me. I was dizzy. I could not remember hardly anything at all.

"Mogul?" I tried to say again, but my voice floated up out of my body and drifted into the air....

Then arms like Commander Reed's arms were lifting me up and carrying me across the fisherman's yard.

And a voice like Mr. Fuller's was telling Selena about the help of the American schooner *Veto*; and how of ninety-three people on board the *Royal Tar*, Captain Reed and his loyal men had rescued almost fifty souls— all of whom might have been lost; and how they had docked at a small wharf here on Isle au Haut; and how the weary survivors were straggling along a road looking for a house when they heard shots ring out in the night.

And Commander Reed's arms were carrying me into the barn joined to the side of the fisherman's small house, and they were setting me down gently in hay, and the hay was warm and soft and sweet just like the hay at home in my barn.

And many others were lying down in the hay around me—the barn was full of survivors from the tragedy of that fateful day—and the old fisherman was bringing people hot broth and basins of water for washing and bedsheets to tear into bandages.

And Selena was cooling my hot forehead with a damp cloth and she was turning me on my side and she was taking the clothes from my back and washing the sharp pain where the bullet had entered my shoulder.

"Mogul?" I tried to ask, reaching out for the friend that had saved my life, the friend I might never see again.

But the kind lady Selena was stroking my hot cheeks with her cool hands and she was holding my head in her lap.

And the Mr. Fuller voice was quietly asking, "Should we go look for the elephant?"

And the Selena voice, thoughtful and concerned, was saying, "It's too dark. He could be miles away by now."

And, as I tried to open my eyes, the Selena face was turning and the Selena voice was saying, "Do you think Kehoe would kill the elephant?"

And the Commander Reed voice was answering sombrely, "Probably. If he got the chance."

And the Selena voice was angry, and she was trembling, and she was saying, "I hope Mogul chases that man right into the sea!"

And there was quiet, and darkness, and warmth, and time was passing by seconds or minutes or hours—it did not matter then.

And the Commander Reed voice was asking Selena, "Do you think Mogul will come back?"

And I felt myself falling deeper and deeper into blackness, farther and farther away from the voices and faces that surrounded me in the barn, into a dream so deep I might never wake from it.

But I struggled to hear the answer to Commander Reed's question. Would Mogul come back? I held my breath. I fought to hear the words.

And the Selena lady was finishing the bandage around my shoulder and she was taking my feverish head from her lap and laying me down in the hay—and I could smell the hay.

"If Mogul is alive," the Selena voice was whispering, "then this is where he'll come."

And gently was she stroking my head.

Chapter Twenty-Six

The hay was soft and warm. It cradled me, held me, stilled me into a deep, deep sleep.

The sweet sharp smell of the hay carried me back to my home, to my pa, to a time when I, a farm boy belonging to Saint John, New Brunswick, rolled and jumped and played in hay, a time long ago when my pa and someone else...oh smell of hay, oh sweet sweet smell of hay...back when my pa and my ma did chores in the barn, and all I had to do was play in hay....

There was a commotion in the fisherman's barn. Other smells broke in upon my smell of hay.

I fought to stay in my hay dreams. No more did I want to smell the stinging salt storm of the sea, acrid fury of the burning ship, bitter poison of Mr. Kehoe's gun, blood smell of fear, of pain, of death...oh smell of hay, and mother's arms, and time before, and ma and pa....

But something would not let me sink once more into the world of sleep and dreams. Something real kept shaking me, waking me, prodding me, poking me...oh mother dear, and time ago, oh smell oh smell of hay....

Still something, someone, shook me—oh smell of blood—would not stop shaking me, waking me...smell of blood and smell of hay....

"It's all right. Everything's going to be just fine," a woman's voice was saying and I struggled to open my heavy eyes.

A woman's face, beautiful as my mother's face was beautiful, but not my mother's face, was floating above me with other faces.

Who were they? And where was I? Was it night or was it day? Was this New Brunswick or was this Maine? Or was this some new world of dreams, beyond all pain and death?

Was Selena alive? My mother, where was she? Commander Reed, was he there? Where oh where was my pa?

And Mogul. Was he dead in a ditch at the side of a road? Or was he chasing—forever through the night to the edges of the world—the evil Mr. Kehoe? Or was Mogul not even real? Was he just a picture on a poster on a tree?

And me? Was I alive? Was the "Amazing New Brunswick Boy with the Magic of Animals in his Blood" real, or had he become a dream?

Was I really lying there in soft sweet hay? Or was I ashes in the seaweed at the bottom of the sea? Or had I perhaps journeyed far beyond death with these faces that floated around me?

What was real, I wondered, and what was dreams? And whose blood was I smelling now?

"We're safe now," the woman's face kept saying. "It's all right now, really it is."

"You've had a rough night," said the face of the man.

I closed my weary eyes. I reached out and squeezed handfuls of the hay. Pointed ends of pieces of hay pricked into my hands. I held handfuls of hay to my nose. I smelled the sweet sharp smell of hay. The hay was real. I lay in hay in a strange barn.

I opened my eyes. I studied the faces above me. My pa and ma were far away. I was on my own in a strange land. But I was not alone. I was among friends. And not all men were like Mr. Kehoe.

It was Commander Reed who was holding me in his arms. It was Selena who gently cooled my forehead with a damp cloth.

I listened. Outside, a wind was still blowing. But we were no longer tossing on the deck of a doomed ship, we were on dry land, safe in the shelter of a barn.

I smelled. There was a fire smell but it was not a fire to fear now. The *Royal Tar* burned no more. Those who had survived the conflagration on the ship now huddled around a small friendly fire outside the door of the barn, drinking tea and getting warm.

And the blood I smelled? It was not my own. It was dried blood mixed with a smell once strange but now so familiar to me; the smell confused me greatly.

I twisted my head back and looked up. An enormous grey shadow stood silently above me. I looked hard at the shape. I did not dare to dream it could be my Mogul.

I was still tired and hot. My lips were dry. Was this just a feverish dream? Was I just imagining this shadow?

"Mogul?" I asked weakly, not even letting myself hope he was really there behind me.

And then, the miracle. The grey shadow reached its

long trunk down to me. I propped myself up on my elbows. The shadow wrapped its trunk around me and squeezed.

The squeeze was no dream. It was real and strong, a squeeze full of life and love.

"Oh Mogul," I said. I reached up for my elephant.

The pain that stabbed through my shoulder was real. And the smile that was on my face then was also oh, so real.

"You're safe, Mogul," I said, and tears flowed down my hot cheeks. "You're alive. You came back to me, Mogul."

Mogul squeezed me again, then gently, gently, he began to lift me from my bed of hay on the floor of the fisherman's barn.

"Be careful, Mogul," Selena said, reaching up for me.

"Let him down," said Commander Reed anxiously.

"Selena. Commander Reed. I'm fine," I said. "Everything is fine."

And so, the elephant, the wild beast from India, the circus star, my brave gentle friend, lifted me up, up, up and set me gently down on his back. I held tight to the familiar thick folds of skin on the elephant's shoulders. I pressed my face against the neck of my elephant friend.

And the mighty Mogul, majestic as a king, walked slowly out of the barn with me teetering on his back.

"Easy," worried Selena.

"Careful," said Commander Reed.

And Mogul marched now, and I propped myself up

and proudly tried to sit erect on his back. We marched out of the barn, out into a new morning, into the yard in front of the fisherman's hut at the edge of the woods and the sea.

He was real, my elephant. Mogul was real and alive and he was there with me. I, too, was alive and real.

Selena and Commander Reed and Mr. Fuller, following right behind us, were real. The joyful bugle-like fanfare that Mr. Jestin made with his voice, with his cheeks puffed out, was real. The cheers of the survivors of the *Royal Tar* for this ragamuffin circus parade led by Mogul and me were real. The triumphant trumpeting sound that Mogul hurled out into the day, chasing Mr. Kehoe and his evil ways away forever was real.

And the love that I felt for Mogul, my elephant friend, and Selena, kind circus lady, and my pa, who would be eagerly waiting for me across the water back in my New Brunswick home—that also was real.

Yes, love was real, I knew, as real as the best dream you could dream.

Love was the best dream of all.

Author's Note

On October 25, 1836, in Penobscot Bay, Maine, the *Royal Tar*, a new steamship from Saint John, New Brunswick, caught fire, burned, and sank. On board were twenty-one crew members, seventy-two passengers "including a number of women and children" and DEXTER'S LOCOMOTIVE MUSEUM AND BURGESS' COLLECTION OF SERPENTS AND BIRDS, a menagerie and circus show that had toured from Boston through Maine and Nova Scotia to New Brunswick.

Thirty-two people and many of the circus animals lost their lives by fire and drowning on that fateful day. Apparently, J. Kehoe, the ship's second engineer, had let the water level in the boilers get too low.

Sixteen of the crew members including Mr. Kehoe— the 'Humane 16' as they were called in the newspapers of the time—deserted the ship with one of the only two lifeboats left on board (the other two having been removed to make room for the elephant). When the other survivors finally landed on Isle au Haut several hours later, they found "the 'Humane 16' very comfortably entertained at Squire Kimball's."

Meanwhile, Captain Thomas Reed and his few remaining crew members—through their courage and perseverance—saved many who would otherwise have perished.

Naturally, there was pandemonium among the circus animals on board the ship. Some died by fire in their cages. Others were backed overboard; at least some of these swam to safety.

There are different accounts of Mogul's fate. It is said that he got off the ship by raising his huge front feet onto the taffrail—just as he raised them in his circus act; the taffrail collapsed and he plunged into the sea. One account reports that "as one of the many instances of the sagacity of the Elephant, it is said, that on hearing the keeper's voice...he turned round [in the water], took him with his trunk back to the boat, where he held on until taken off by one of the boats."

It is said by some that Mogul died hours later while swimming in the sea. I prefer the story of a nameless farmer on Brice's Island who came out into his field one morning in October to discover an elephant calmly eating his haystack.

And the boy? In the list of those who sailed on the *Royal Tar* that fateful day in October, 1836, are many adults—mostly named—and several nameless "boys" (ship's boys, circus boys, passenger boys) including "a boy belonging to Halifax, N.S." For me, the boy in this book, the simple farm boy from New Brunswick who missed his mother, loved animals and wanted to go to sea, is one of those "boys"..."a boy belonging to Saint John, New Brunswick."

Printed in Canada